Ann +

Merry Christmas!!

Maggie.

Oulipo Canada: Book One

An Anthology by Northumberland Writers

Edited by Michael Hanlon

© Published by Joceeloo, 2013
Cobourg, ON, Canada
jocee@joceeloo.com

ISBN: 978-0-9920946-0-7

*For more information about Oulipo Canada,
please contact jocee@joceeloo.com*

Cover and book design by Jocelyn MacLean

Oulipo Canada
Book One

1.	Welcome	Michael Hanlon	xx
2.	Hope	Mary Soni	1
3.	Framboise	Christine Sharp	7
4.	A Himalayan Childhood	Margaret Bain	13
5.	Pure Grama	Ann Partridge	18
6.	Santa Came to My House on Christmas Eve .... Heidi Croot		25
7.	The Snow Plough	Carole Payne	33
8.	Cacotopia	Michael Hanlon	38
9.	The Bone Doctor and the Undercover Patient .... Lori Pearson		45
10.	A Canadian Winter's Tale	Margaret Bain	48
11.	Life, Death and Resurrection	Mary Fleming	50
12.	Freedom 55	Ann Partridge	53
13.	A Good Listener	Laura MacCourt	61
14.	Love At:	Lori Pearson	66
15.	Elegy	Lori Pearson	68
16.	Finding Arthur (excerpt)	Carole Payne	70
17.	Netless	Ann Partridge	76
18.	Autumn	Lori Pearson	82
19.	From Bernardo Boy to Man of Leisure .... Ellen Curry		83
20.	A Learning Experience	Mary Soni	87
21.	Angels Among Us	Lori Pearson	94
22.	IMBY	Lori Pearson	95

23. A Trickle of Words about Writer's Block
   ....Jocelyn MacLean 98
24. Why You are Loved ....Lori Pearson   100
25. 150 Word Topics 103
   i. Voice on the Stair 104
   ii. Siblings 107
   iii. Time 109
   iv. The Senses 110
   v. Starlight 112
   vi. Awaiting Evening's Peace 113
   vii. Arnold Raced from the Room 114
   viii. Touch 116
   ix. On Choosing a Name 118
   x. The Traveler 120
   xi. Breakfast with Charles 121
   xii. Suspect One 122
   xiii. Ides of March 124
   xiv. Lullaby of Snow 125
26. The Girl in the Emerald Bikini
    A Progressive Story 126
27. About the Oulipo Writers
    Margaret Bain 134
    Heidi Croot 135
    Ellen Curry 137
    Mary Fleming 138
    Michael Hanlon 139
    Laura MacCourt 140
    Jocelyn MacLean 142
    Ann Partridge 143
    Carole Payne 144
    Lori Pearson 145
    Christine Sharp 146
    Mary Soni 147

Welcome

What is Oulipo Canada? It's a gathering of Northumberland writers who meet regularly to talk about anything to do with writing, even if it's only something on a postcard. In short, anything that can be set down in words.

The name comes from that of a somewhat similar organization in France: Ouvroir de la Littérature Potentielle. Now that's quite *une bouchée*. In English it's Workshop for Potential Literature. Wopolit didn't have much of a ring so we stuck with Oulipo, which, after all, is in one of our official languages.

We've been meeting twice a month since the beginning of the year to talk about searching for the perfect word and trying to form beautiful sentences and paragraphs and sometimes whole stories. We write short pieces, long pieces, poems, anecdotes, memoirs, character studies, riddles, romances, mysteries, travel stories, tales of adventure, remorse, hope, joy, fear, courage.

Some of what we do can be found in this anthology, our first. You'll find some short pieces under the heading "Topics." These come from a challenge we give ourselves at the end of each meeting: to go away and write no more than 150 words suggested by a particular topic. We've done 150-worders on Time, Why I Write, The Hottest Week in Eternity, Give It Up, Siblings, Breakfast With Charles, Arnold Raced From the Room, and Choosing a Name.

Try it for yourself. Try writing 150 words suggested by, say, A Swim in the Lake, Your Neighbour's Hedge, Raccoons, A Sandcastle, or Ice Cream. Keep it tight. Make every word count. You might even enjoy the challenge.

And we hope you enjoy our anthology.

Michael Hanlon

Hope

By Mary Soni

I almost had a kid last year. She died before she was even born. Oh well, I would have been a terrible mom anyway. I decided to call her Hope, before I even knew if it was a girl. See, I never really had much hope in my life; I was born dirt poor, stayed dirt poor, am dirt poor. My brothers and sisters and I, we were always the bad kids, the rowdy out-of-control kids. The kids everybody was always watching out for, always saying "Watch out for that brood – ain't a good one in the lot of them. No hope for any of them, if you ask me." And that suited us fine. We fought, we cut class, tormented other kids. . .basically did whatever we wanted, whenever we wanted to do it. Our parents didn't care; dad ran off, mom just ignored us. I don't think she really wanted kids.

When we got older, we smoked and drank and partied every night of the week. I don't think any of us made it to high school. And we didn't care either. We wouldn't have gone even if they did let us in. We'd lost track of how many times people said how hopeless we were. And of course then there were the drugs – you could get any kind of drug you wanted at one of our parties. Sometimes we'd see high school kids hanging around a party, trying to pretend like they were all bad and wild – and then one of us would challenge them to do shots or something and before you knew it, they'd either be passed out or being dragged out the door puking their guts out. And then we'd roll our eyes and laugh.

Eventually we drifted apart; some got married or moved to some other town. We all found new crowds, and none of us ever grew up. Eventually some of the married ones had kids and tried to make it seem like they were cleaning up, going straight. Yeah, right – at least I knew what went on when nobody was looking.

I eventually ended up in some nameless, faceless big city, where I didn't know a soul and nobody ever really knew me. I shacked up in whatever dive had a free bed – or, more often than not, someone willing to share one. I never knew anyone's name, and I doubt they ever knew mine.

By day, I drifted through the streets like a ghost – swipe a donut here, grab a coffee there. I had no job, so not much money. But what little I got my hands on I ran through like it was water. Never really had anything to show for it, though. Sometimes I just liked to sit, and watch the world go by. And sometimes I could actually do it without attracting nasty glares from all the rich snobs walking by me. Not that it bothered me – I didn't think any of them really saw me; I was just yet another symbol of a growing epidemic nobody ever wants to admit is real. (Oh well – screw them, what do I care? Just means it's time to go find another party, another bed to crash in – hopefully I'll find one and won't have to sleep outside; it's getting closer to winter and colder every day.)

Sometimes I'd wait till late at night, scrounge up a few bucks, then get on the subway and ride till the end of the line – it's warmer than outside, even if I can't stay all night. If I got really lucky and had enough cash left over from my day, I'd book a cheap motel room and for one night pretend I was normal, not some strung out junkie drunk always looking for the next big party, the next fix, the next score.

My hair has been many different colours over the years – just one more way to abuse my body: throw a different chemical on my head every week. I've been blonde, black, brown, red, blue, green, orange, pink, purple, yellow – just about every colour under the sun, and sometimes more than one colour at a time. Some friends think it's cool, others have told me I need to calm it down – I don't listen to any of them, I just go by my mood on any given day. Once or twice I've even shaved my hair completely off, and other times I've gone years without cutting it, so that it grows so long I can tuck it into my jeans. I had it really long and dyed like a rainbow once. But then my hair started coming out in my brush, too many chemicals, so I shaved it all off, to hell with it, it'll grow back.

    I'm like that with everything. I have no attachment to anything. I found a cat once, eating out of a dumpster, thought it was cute and took it home with me. I was staying with this guy at the time — he had a nice apartment — but if anyone came over I couldn't leave the bedroom (usually I climbed out the window and went back later). So I take this cat home and try to clean it up and feed it, and the guy comes home and he's horrified, screaming about me messing up his apartment. He says if I want to stay, the cat goes, and I hesitated for a minute so he slaps me across the face – the cat ran off and so did I, but not till the guy was very, very sorry. I never bothered to look for that cat though, 'cause what did I care if it came back? It could be road-kill for all I care.

    I thought I saw my dad once, walking down the street. He looked good, like he had lots of money. I never knew if it was him but I thought I saw a glimmer of recognition when he looked up at me as we passed each other – I ran back and spat in his face. I hope it was him and that he remembered who I was after that.

    I've never really had any friends, just people I partied with, or shared a bed with. And sometimes sharing that bed would cost me more than a motel room would've cost. But like I said, what did I care? I just kept living and partying and never let anything bug me. There was this one woman, a nurse, that pretended to care when I almost had the kid, but when Hope died, she stopped coming around. A lot of people stopped coming around when Hope died.

I never really wanted a kid. It was just one of those things – I'd been sharing a bed with someone, but when he found out he kicked me out, that's how much he wanted a kid. So there I am wandering the streets, got this kid growing inside me, what am I supposed to do now? But then I remember, there's this nurse who works at this soup kitchen I sometimes go to, maybe she can help. So I go look her up and I tell her and she's all happy and full of information, not realizing that the only info I want is on how to get rid of this thing, and she gives me her card with an address, date and time written on it and says come to my office, we'll talk.

I get there and immediately I know I'm in the wrong place, it's all nice and clean and rich people are everywhere, and I'm just a dumb street rat, I can see it in their eyes. But then the nurse comes out and pulls me inside before I can leave, and she's handing me all these pamphlets and papers. Her eyes dim when I pointedly hold up the one on termination, and I can see it, she's trying to save my soul or something, or maybe she just cares about the kid. Then she pulls one out on adoption, and I know it's all about the kid. She says that to end it would cost money, and I know I don't have any. Then she says that some people will pay a lot of money for a healthy kid, and if I took care of myself and the kid came out OK, I could use the money for a new start, a new life. I roll my eyes – who is she kidding, what new life could I ever have? But the money does sound good so I ask how much, and when she tells me I definitely decide to go that route, but where am I going to stay while I do this thing, can't sleep on the streets and have a healthy kid. So she puts me up in a cheap motel, tells me to stay there till it's born, then I can use the money to move somewhere nice.

It actually starts to go good after that: I sleep when I want and eat when I want and sit around watching TV all day. I start to think that maybe I've found a good thing here; I can just make people babies and live off all the rich snobs the rest of my life. But after a while I get bored, those old itches come back. I'm almost starting to show a little now, and I've called her Hope – but I'm alone all the time now, too much time to think, so I go walking, and I find some of my old gang, and we end up trashing the motel room and getting kicked out – but I don't care, I'm having a blast, screw the consequences and somebody get me a beer, or a shot, or a smoke, or something. Next thing I know I'm in some hospital somewhere, and they're saying I OD'd on something – I can't remember what, and the baby's gone, couldn't survive in the toxic stew I created.

The next few days are a blur – the nurse coming in, looking at me with disappointed eyes, saying what a shame it was but I knew she didn't care, she was just mad 'cause she had to pay off the motel guy. Doctors and nurses and cleaners and who knew who else coming in and out of the room. People visiting the chump in the next bed, but nobody notices me. Then somebody decides they need the space so I'm back out on the streets. And I have nothing but the irony of it all – all my life people said I had no hope, and then I finally have Hope growing inside me, and I kill it.

The days turn into weeks and I still haven't gone looking for another party. Then it's been months, and I still haven't been back. I have no idea what's holding me back, except for maybe I don't want to die, I'm afraid that the next party might actually kill me. So I stay locked in my shell, bouncing from shelter to shelter. And I see people I used to party with and they all ask me to come out with them and I ignore everybody. Then finally, it's been a year, one whole year, no parties, no drugs, no drinks, no nothing, just me. But the problem with being clean is all the memories, everything that got chased away by all the shit that I took, drank, whatever, it all comes running back. And I don't know what it is about this night, maybe it's all been building up, or maybe it's just 'cause I know it's a year ago today that Hope died, but it finally seems too much. I don't know if I can do this anymore. I'm sitting here in this shitty room, just like all the other shelters, wondering where to go from here.

I notice that some kid left their diary, and a pen, and I pick them up. I read all about this kid's hopes and dreams and it makes me kinda sad. But there's a bunch of empty space and the kid ain't coming back here so I check if the pen works and start to write. About Hope, and about the past, and about everything. I scribble down everything I can think of, don't really know why, maybe I just figure if it's all written down, I can put it away somewhere, just put it in a box, or bury it, or burn it, or something, to avoid looking at it. To try and forget it all. Nope, sorry, too painful, can't deal, just throw it out, move on, don't look at it now. I don't know if it will work. But I've spent all night writing and someone's gonna come kick us out soon, the sun's almost up. I better finish this soon. I don't know if I'll keep the diary, or just leave it here for someone else. Maybe I'll leave it here. It's probably already too late for me, but maybe someone else will read it, and maybe for them – there's still hope.

Framboise

By Christine Sharp

From the basement storage area, I carried up dusty boxes containing half-empty bottles of crème de menthe, Cherry Heering, apricot brandy, absurdly-flavoured schnapps (green apple and maple among them) and other peculiar liqueurs, representing key ingredients of every fad cocktail of the previous ten years, and segregated them into a category which the bar staff and I quickly dubbed "duds."

I held up an orb-shaped bottled, girdled with gold-painted plastic, and shook my head. "Framboise!?" Hundreds of dollars had been invested in this kind of stuff. I dampened a bar rag and tried to wipe the dust and sticky residue off each bottle.

"We'll have to figure out a way to get rid of all this," I said to Cynthia, our resident "mixologist." "Start looking up cocktail recipes. We'll put on some specials during intermission bar services and try to blow it out of here."

The first production of the summer season was "Shirley Valentine."

I worked late in my office nearly every evening and often made a habit of wandering down to the lobby at intermission to get a sense of the crowd's reaction. During almost every performance, at least one theatregoer would walk out, offended by the raunchiness of Shirley's monologue.

One night the phone on my desk rang. One of the bartenders was calling. "You should come down here. Someone is ordering framboise!"

I ran downstairs, almost giddy. This I had to see.

I met Cynthia in the doorway. "They've asked for cream – I'm going to the kitchen."

Standing by the bar, in the pose of waiting, were two well-dressed, well-coiffed, and well-perfumed middle-aged ladies, wearing chunky jewellery and hand-painted silk scarves, the accoutrements of good salaries and disposable incomes, and enough free time to spend afternoons poking through artisan-created collectibles.

"Did one of you happen to order the framboise?" I asked.

"Yes," they both responded brightly.

"Both of us are having it," said one.

I introduced myself as the manager. "We are all intrigued," I said, "as it's not often that someone orders framboise."

At that moment, Cynthia returned with a fresh carton of half-and-half in her hand.

"Perfect," one of the women said.

"How would you like this served?" Cynthia asked.

The other answered, "If you could just get me a spoon, I'll pour it myself and show you how it's done."

Cythnia placed a brandy snifter, spoon, cream, and the framboise on the counter.

"You put the cream in the glass first," the woman said. "Then, if you carefully pour the liqueur over the back of the spoon, it will make a pattern, just like a peppermint swirl candy."

Cynthia and I leaned inward to watch. The woman turned the spoon backward and carefully poured.

"Oh!" we gasped as the deep red liquid merged with the cream in dark ribbons. "How beautiful," I said, "that must take practise."

"Yes," the woman said, smiling, "a bit." She then poured a second equally beautiful drink for her friend.

She held hers up to her mouth and then paused. "Would you like to try it?"

She thrust the glass towards me with both hands, as if offering me a communion chalice. "Just take a sip. I'll drink from the other side."

"Seriously?"

"Yes, go ahead, try it."

So I did. It was very pleasant.

At that moment, we noticed a party of six, dressed in their coats, evenings still being chilly, leaving the theatre, with the hunched-over look of escapees, trying to be discreet yet creating a breeze in their haste to depart.

"They obviously don't like the show," the woman mentioned.

"It's the word 'clitoris.' It sends them running, particularly the men."

"I can't imagine walking out of any show, no matter how much I disliked it. Have you ever walked out of anything?"

It surprised me to answer "yes." Yes, I had and I had forgotten about it.

She looked at me expectantly.

"It was during 'Waiting for Godot.' I know it's a classic and that many people think it's funny, but I can't sit through it. And I have tried. I have gone to several different productions of it. I even saw it presented as a ballet. But there is one point that I cannot get beyond."

The woman took a step backwards and cocked her head, appraising me. I noticed how well manicured were the fingers that coiled around her glass, the contents of which were now the colour and consistency of Pepto-Bismal. Each nail looked as sleek, shiny, and hard as a cherry cough lozenge.

I have always battled tension in my upper chest, neck and face. I could feel the tightening begin.

"I know what point that was," she said definitively. "The rope around the neck," she declared.

"Yes," I replied almost with relief. "That's it! As soon as one character puts a rope around the neck of another, I have to leave! There's nothing else that I know of that has that same effect on me." I inadvertently touched my hand to my throat. I could feel a hint, a physical memory, of a rope, and of the roiling sensation in my gut that would drive me running from the theatre.

She stepped back even further. Surrounding us was a sea of people, laughing, with tinkling voices, and sparkling glassware in their hands. They seemed, unconsciously, to accommodate her as she moved backwards, away from me.

She shifted her glass from her right hand to her left. Her voice took on an accusatory tone. "You have an issue with anything being tight around your neck, don't you. Scarves, necklaces, anything, don't you."

Yes, in fact I did. I couldn't stand to have anything tight around my neck. I remember wrenching and stretching the turtlenecks that my mother tried to dress me in, until they sagged like gunnysacks draped around my collarbones.

My nausea suddenly became real and fully blown.

She slowly stretched her right arm out straight, with her first finger extended, while every ounce of conviviality drained from her face. Her nail gleamed. "You were hung by the neck in a previous life," she proclaimed loudly. "You were hung by the neck in a previous life!"

I felt like I had taken a sharp blow to the chest. The words were crystal clear – a pronouncement, then a condemnation.

I tried to spit out words but nothing came. I couldn't catch my breath.

A gong was sounding. Intermission was over. Everyone started moving towards the theatre. The woman and her friend disappeared into the jostling crowd.

I spotted her glass on the corner of the bar, heavily rimmed in lipstick, a half-inch of pinkish liquid remaining, redolent of pus mixed with blood.

Is this what is meant by "bad karma"? Is this why I had a compulsion as a child to run into Catholic churches and light candles? Am I guilty? Am I doomed? Am I damned?

I went to my office, turned off the computer and lights, and grabbed my coat to leave. I could hear the audience laughing uproariously, and the shrill, chirping voice of the actress playing "Shirley" rising above it like a descant.

At 7:00 a.m. the next day, I had my regular chiropractic appointment with Dr. S. for my standard neck "adjustment"; a quick snap, crackle, and a pop, and I would usually be done. I sat in a hospital gown on the stainless steel table, swinging my legs back and forth, as I waited.

When he first took me on as a patient, he made me go for x-rays. Sure enough, there was an obvious crook in my neck, apparent from every angle, the same crook Dr. H. had noticed back in Cobourg, the same crook that constantly made my head tilt to the right side, and had caused my mother no end of anxiety. "For god's sake, hold your head up straight," she would hiss. And I would cry, "But I am. I am!" Congenital, the two chiropractors had concurred.

The doctor stepped in briskly, wearing a brilliantly white coat, exuding energy, health, and all-round well-being.

"I have something to tell you," I said immediately. I reminded him about my x-rays, and then relayed what happened the night before. I told him exactly what the woman had said, and that I would never forget that finger – that finger thrust directly at my face.

As he listened, his features seemed to harden, and his mouth tightened.

When I finished, he looked intently at me, his deep brown eyes mere inches from my own. In a soft, unusually low voice, he said, "I don't think I can treat you today."

He, too, stepped back a foot. I felt a twinge of panic.

He sputtered. "It's too funny!" He leaned forward in a feeble attempt to touch me, then backed off, nearly doubled over in laughter, that I realized now, he had obviously been trying to suppress. Tears formed at the corners of his eyes.

He placed a hand on my shoulder. It radiated warmth. "Come back tomorrow," he laughed. "Come back tomorrow and we'll try again."

A Himalayan Childhood

By Margaret Bain

I must have been a bloodthirsty child. One of my favourite books at the age of seven was "Man-eaters of the Kumaon" by the legendary tiger-hunter Jim Corbett, full of ghastly tales of sleeping children snatched from their beds and farm labourers ambushed in the tall elephant-grass. We lived in India, the land of the tiger, then. In hot, sweaty, steaming Calcutta most of the time but in deliciously cool Darjeeling in the blistering summers. In these last days of the British Raj, summer in Calcutta was considered insupportable for white women and children, so after the first really hot days when we all got prickly heat and drove our mothers crazy with our misery, we would pile into the old, asthmatic puffing-billies and chug northwards, in swirling clouds of acrid black engine-smoke, up the dusty foothills to the cool tea plantations of Darjeeling.

We had sleeping-berths in the train, my sister and I squabbling for the top bunk, so close to the ceiling — "It's MY turn now!" "No it's not, you had it last time." "Oh, it's SO unfair!" The itchy wool blankets were ideal for making a secret fortress to read in by flashlight, to weave imaginary quests and adventures. I used to get up early before the others were awake and sneak out to stand in the narrow, gently-rocking corridor to watch the great orange globe of the sun rise slowly over dry fields and spindly trees in the hazy morning mist. The endless "tapokka-tapokka tapokka-tapokka" of the train wheels spoke of adventure and faraway places and settled in some deep, elemental part of my brain. To this day, when I'm stopped at a level-crossing on one of the lakeshore roads, I always wind down my window to hear once again that long-ago voice of the train wheels as the container-cars lumber by.

In Darjeeling we lived in a large, crumbling compound looking down steep hillsides to the wide, green tea plantations, dotted with brilliant specks of orange, red, and yellow — the dozens of slim, weather-beaten, sari-clad women endlessly pinching out the fresh new tips of the tea bushes, their deft fingers flying so fast they were just a blur. Magic happened at dawn. North of us were the greatest mountains in the world, the Himalayas, and Kanchenjunga was one of the highest of them all. Only visible across the misty valleys in the very first light of day, the gigantic mountain, palest pink, hundreds of miles away, filled the whole sky, so enormous that I had to tip my head backwards to see its peak, before it vanished into the haze.

My sister and I went to school on rugged little mountain ponies, my favourite called Sikkim Jimmy after the tiny Himalayan kingdom on the borders of Tibet. The ponies were rented like taxicabs by smiling-faced, strong young Tibetan women wearing long woollen skirts and brightly striped aprons of scarlet, green, and blue. They would run beside us, bare-footed, for mile after mile whatever the weather, laughing and calling to each other. Once out of sight of waving mothers and ayahs, however, these mischievous girls took huge delight in poking their ponies with sharp sticks, doubling over with laughter as the little memsahibs' feet flew out of the stirrups and we were left, fingers desperately twined in coarse tangled manes, hanging on grimly, while the sprinting ponies seemed to enjoy the fun as much as their owners. We never once told our parents, of course.

I loved the noisy, cheerful chaos of the weekly market in Darjeeling, its rickety stalls overflowing with custard apples and fresh mangos, braying livestock, sticky sweetmeats, jewel-coloured silk saris, towering stacks of tin cans. Leather-faced Tibetan women sold great piles of wool, the skeins dyed with vegetable extracts in thrilling colours. My absolute favourite was a deep, deep purple, but my mother said very firmly that that was a colour for old ladies, not children, so I never got the purple sweater I longed for. Prices varied widely depending on who I was with – carrying the shopping-basket for my mother, everything was surprisingly expensive. With my mother and my ayah more dickering was done and money saved; but if I went with my ayah, Jheti, and the cook, Hanif, prices melted away as he strutted and shouted his importance and got his way.

    I was an impossible toddler, pushing daisies up my nose (and having to go to the hospital), chewing on jagged leaves that made my tongue spout terrifying fountains of bright red blood (the hospital again), tumbling headfirst down the steep, stony garden paths and cutting my head open (hospital again – and again), obsessively popping the buds on all the fuchsia bushes before the flowers had a chance to open (no hospital this time but stern lectures from an infuriated neighbour). My worst transgression, though, occurred one day when a rabid dog wandered into the compound – all the women and children were ordered indoors while the men of the community gathered together with sticks and staves to chase off, probably to try to kill, the unfortunate animal. As the men rounded the corner of the main building, driving the slavering mad dog before them, out I toddled, straight into its path. My father rushed forward, grabbed hold of me and threw me in the nearest door he could open. Then my mother descended on me, so terrified at what might have happened that she seized a hairbrush and spanked me thoroughly with the bristly side, leaving me sobbing in a great big rattan chair. I can still hear the doleful creaking of the dusty old chair as I lay there, shifting about in some pain, uncomforted by the soft cushions, alone in the big cold room. But I did deserve it.

It was wartime, of course, so I'm not quite sure why my father, who had been drafted into the Indian Army, was in Darjeeling at all but presumably he had had a spell of leave. We had been bombed by Japanese planes in Calcutta, sheltering in rat-infested dugouts one Christmas Eve, but the main signs of the war in Darjeeling were the whoops and hollers of the American GIs sent there for some R&R, so bored with the limited local social scene that they would commandeer the little Tibetan ponies and race them round the quiet streets, often sitting backwards in their saddles, hanging on to the disgruntled pony's tail. We had a limited variety of the food that our fellow Brits were used to, especially dairy products, and an x-ray of my leg many years later showed the dark lines, like close-together rings on a tree stump, that indicate the retarded growth of mild malnutrition. For some reason, our only butter came from tins labelled "Brown and Polson," the name indelibly etched on my mind, for when opened, there was a mass of yellow goo swimming in evil-looking dark brown fluid – I think we would have preferred yak butter. It wasn't easy for my mother to keep us supplied with children's books to read, either. One day she famously heard me reading out loud in my bedroom, very slowly and very carefully, and knowing my reading was better than that, came through to find me lying flat on my stomach on my bed, peering down at a book on the floor below me, reading it upside-down because I was so bored with reading the same few stories over and over again!

The distant war impinged on me more and more as I grew older and could listen to the radio and perhaps even read the occasional newspaper. One dreadful day I was old enough to feel horror at a broadcast carrying news from North Africa that the Allies had suffered such overwhelming casualties that they had had to request a day's ceasefire to bury their dead. No one has been able to tell me for sure which battle this was, but

I've never forgotten the childish dread I felt at those harrowing words, the helpless feeling that the world was coming to a terrible end. My Himalayan childhood may have had some of these dark moments, but I feel incredibly privileged to have so many, still amazing memories of my summer days among those magnificent mountains.

Pure Grama

By Ann Partridge

The clean scent of Ivory soap takes me back to the bathroom of my grandmother's house. I remember kneeling and running my hands over the surprising feel of grittiness when immersed in her old bathtub. It wasn't smoothly finished like the ones I was used to. I always checked for sand again during my first bath on every visit. There never was any, because going to the beach wasn't one of Grama's activities.

Down a dimly-lit hallway from the bathroom was the centre of Grama's house – the kitchen. The hallway was crowded with boxes of canned goods and I still remember staring in wonder at a whole case of Kraft peanut butter.

The dominant feature of the kitchen was a long table covered with a red-and-white checked vinyl tablecloth. On special occasions she used a white linen tablecloth and produced bottles of wine. In the centre against the wall was a wooden lazy Susan containing a wide variety of condiments and napkins in a wooden holder. When I learned what that round piece of hardware was called, I turned my head for a sharp glance at my cousin Susan, who I thought might be insulted by the moniker. She showed no offence, but I was thereafter on guard for a negatively named device with my name on it.

My grandmother always sat at one end of the kitchen table in a wooden chair that backed against the wall, so that she was facing the centre of the room. That is where I remember her greeting me and pulling me into her enveloping bosom where once again I inhaled Ivory soap and a hint of something sharp I later identified as bleach. Grama didn't seem to have breasts; it was more like one continual bolster that provided comfort once the initial fear of suffocation passed. In the summer, both the bathroom and Gram's bosom would add powder to their bouquets.

My mother also had a prominent, more pointed bosom, but she didn't gather me into it. Contact with Mom's breasts was limited to inadvertent bumping when I was in the way and they seemed more the consistency of a shoulder than a pillow.

My grandmother always wore dresses. I think she called them house dresses. They were often flowered or patterned, but she would wear solid colours to go to an important event like a wedding or funeral. She often wore an apron around her waist. In warm weather she would lift it up and fan herself with it. She didn't wear pantyhose, but knee-high nylon-coloured stockings that were often rolled below her knees, which were swollen, shiny and smoothly white.

Always occupying a designated spot in her kitchen corner was Gram's purse. When away from home, she was always asking, "Now, where did I put my bag?" It was black, and the size of a small sports bag, full of compartments and attachments. Gram was always rummaging in her bag. She might have a plastic folder containing newspaper articles she wanted to show you, a pair of stockings she was knitting, a collection of rings on a large safety pin or pliers that she could always find handy.

Grama looked at life through thick pop-bottle lenses. Her glasses magnified her chocolate-brown eyes which seemed to see right into me. She never regarded me for long periods of time, but her gaze felt both knowing and approving.

From her habitual corner of the kitchen Gram held court. Family and friends gathered on chairs around the table and relayed the latest happenings. She would nod often and slap her thighs if something struck her as funny. Her laughter seemed to burst out of her throat and its rollicking rumble would often echo from the others seated nearby.

If someone told her a piece of bad news, she would pat her bosom repeatedly while saying, "Oh, oh, oh!" It was almost as if she was willing her heart to keep pumping. If it was dire information, she would rock forward and backwards in her chair.

The kitchen was the centre of Gram's house for a reason. She would never say, "I love you." Her way of showing you was to feed you.

And she never did it by halves. In the morning, even if there were only four people in the house, she would boil a dozen eggs. My job was to make a big stack of toast and butter it. Real butter – she always had a full pound in her butter dish and told me not to scrimp when slathering it on. She would cook a full pound of bacon and for some reason always had a whole head of lettuce, sliced in half on the table and the proverbial big block of old cheddar cheese. There would be at least three kinds of jam, marmalade, peanut butter and sliced tomatoes if they were in season. A pot of tea was a constant.

It took quite some time to do this large meal the justice that Gram expected, what with a full tumbler of milk and all. She didn't approve of just a piece of toast and peanut butter. I would eat until it was a great relief to get up and gather the dishes to be washed. She had a step stool I could stand on to reach the sink. Bewailing the lack of appetites, she would bustle around clearing everything away, while I washed and dried the dishes. My diligence pleased her. I could put the silverware away, but couldn't reach the cupboards to replace the plates and cups.

It seemed like not long after this procedure was complete, that she would begin to plan what to have for lunch. She liked to serve "cold cuts" and many of the familiar elements of breakfast. When I got older, I learned to sleep in to miss one of the non-stop feedings.

At noon Gram would turn on the radio to hear the news and then turn it off again when it was over. She would mull over news items that were pertinent to her. Not politics, but accidents, fires or anything affecting people she knew. The only television I ever saw her watch was the news. The rest of the programming was meaningless to her.

My sister and I would often visit our grandmother in the summer when we were out of school. She would direct us to clear out her front flower bed. Looking back, I think her swollen knees didn't bend well. I remember the feel of the rough surface of her front cement "stoop" on the back of my short-clad legs while we observed her planting ritual. Holding on to the piece of metal pipe that served for a railing on the step, I remember my hands smelled like dirt and rust.

Carrying a handled basket like you can buy peaches in, Gram just sprinkled a large variety of unidentified seeds that she had saved from last year's garden. I imagine she had once fed chickens with the same motions. She would laugh while she was doing it, imagining what the results would be in the coming weeks.

Once she walked us a couple of blocks away to visit her sister-in-law in her tiny, shiny home. Unlike our grandmother, our great aunt was a clean fanatic. Even her lamp shades had plastic on them. My main memory of the visit is the back of my short-clad legs sticking to the plastic that covered her chesterfield. Every time I moved, the suction sound of my legs unsticking drew sharp glances from my elderly unfamiliar relative. Her floors were so polished that my sister slipped in her sock feet and fell on her back in the sparkling kitchen. Grama didn't approve of bare feet. Socks and shoes were mandatory.

When the endless, tortuous visit ended and we were walking back to the friendly clutter of Gram's house, she observed, "Did you see her dinner on the stove? There was one sausage and one potato in the pan. Hmph."

In between meals, if not much was happening, Gram would relax in her customary corner chair in the kitchen with a paring knife in her hand. She liked to cut up things to eat. She never just picked up an apple and bit into it. She cut off pieces one at a time and ate them. Often she would have the big brick of old cheese in front of her and cut a slice at a time with the paring knife and eat it while pondering what to make next.

When I roll out pie dough, the tender texture and distinctive oily pastry smell takes me back to Gram's kitchen. Her paring knife would fly when she peeled and cored apples. She would give me my own lump of dough to mould with my hands into a shape to fit into a small aluminum pie plate. The clinging scent of tart apples and dough would later mingle with cinnamon and my mouth would water when the deep dish of golden goodness would emerge from the oven.

When we stayed at our grandmother's, bedtime took getting used to on each visit. Her pillows, like her bosom, were more substantial than what we were used to. Her bedding, like her clothes, held a faint whiff of bleach mixed with a linen closet mustiness. Once the lights went out at night time, they didn't go back on until morning. More than once I was startled by a shining light bobbing in the dark hallway outside the partially open bedroom door. Gram used a flashlight when she needed to get up in the night.

Then there was her deep buzz-saw snoring. It was as distinctive as her laugh, but took time to get used to. If we stayed more than a few days, it became a loud lullaby – like the sound of waves striking the shore.

Grama kept her photographs in a suitcase crammed in the back of her bedroom closet. I wondered if it was in case of disaster, it would be the first thing she would salvage. She didn't clarify, when I asked. Like a treasure chest, once unearthed, every single element needed to be evaluated and commented on. We spent many afternoons examining family connections in pictures.

She once pulled a handgun out of that same deep closet when her nephew, "that crazy Black Harvey," showed up at her door intoxicated and belligerent. She did manage to send him on his way and after I recovered from my shock, she showed me that while he was obviously loaded, the gun was not.

I have quite a few younger cousins, and occasionally a number of them would spend time with our grandmother. She loved to get hold of the babies and rock them in her old oak rocker with the leather seat. The rocker was in front of the kitchen window facing the back yard. The light softened Gram's face while the chair creaked in a life-enhancing rhythm. She never looked happier.

When some of the older kids would get into a squabble, Gram never yelled at them. She would wait a minute or two for them to figure it out and if they didn't she would pour water over them. It was surprisingly effective.

For my grandmother's ninetieth birthday, family members rented a hall to mark the occasion. Now, she knew it was her birthday, but she didn't know what the plan was. One of my aunts told her she was taking her out to lunch and then delivered her for everyone to surprise.

After standing and patiently greeting a long line of well-wishers, Gram began her regular refrain, "Where did I put my bag?" When it was located, and she was seated, she unzipped, what I thought was a larger than normal bag, and from its depths she drew out a bottle of wine, a sleeve of Styrofoam cups and a big block of old cheddar cheese. She laughed in delight at our expressions and we echoed her merriment.

One of the last meetings I had with my grandmother before she became ill was at a casino. She wanted to go and a few family members arranged for half a dozen of us to meet up there. It surprised me that she was very nonchalant playing the slots. She had a walker then and she would wheel it over to a machine, sit on the walker's seat and press the buttons and levers for a few minutes and then calmly get up and move on. I had thought that a ninety-some-year-old woman would be dazzled by the lights, automated non-stop ringing sounds and crowds of people.

But Gram didn't show much emotion until after we had lined up for the buffet luncheon. After filling her plate with a wide assortment of foodstuffs and settling herself at the table surrounded by family with similarly full plates she looked around and nodded without saying anything. Then she broke out in a big beaming smile that would have done justice to winning the jackpot.

Santa Came to My House on Christmas Eve

By Heidi Croot

Santa came to my house on Christmas Eve, as he did every year, finding our bungalow effortlessly, that small brown house on Sunray Crescent in Lambeth, Ontario, flying across the night sky behind his reindeer, bells jingling, his red-lacquered sleigh shining from the light of the stars, bearing packages hand-picked for me.

My imagination stoked to crescendo by my mother through her conspiratorial glances, her dramatic consulting with her watch and redoubled efforts on her work in the kitchen as if time were running short, her dramatic "shh" as she stopped her task, holding her index finger aloft as she listened intently to mysterious noises outside in the gathering dusk, somehow beyond my range of hearing—"What was that?"— I could do naught but spend my afternoon fretting about Santa's fallibility and the prospect of him arriving before we were ready. But, year after year, the jolly old man's timing was impeccable. He never showed up until after we'd eaten dinner and washed the dishes.

The house was filled with the savoury smell of stuffed turkey, sweet mashed turnip, rotkraut with apple, and my mother's incomparable Yorkshire puddings, rising three and a half inches high in the muffin tin, golden, steaming, glazed with hot oil, their deep creamy centres an invitation to her silken gravy, the mood in the kitchen becoming tense and chaotic as the completion of all dishes coalesced around those 12 perfect masterpieces, my father and I meek, obedient, willing, for once, to take orders: "Keith, where's the big platter? Heidi, hand me that spoon. Stir this, please—and do not let it boil. Did you hear me? Put the salt and pepper on the table. Keep that turkey warm—why haven't you covered it with foil? Where's the gravy boat? Did you warm it?"

It was full dark outside by the time we sat down to eat at our Emily Post table, each of the four big windows at front and back fogged with condensation, preventing me from keeping a proper lookout, insulating us within our festivities. The halo of buttery light from two tall taper candles in their silver holders in the centre of the round table encircled the three of us and Mops, our beloved black, white and brown terrier, sitting attentively in his own chair pulled close to join the family, though, to his chagrin, stopped short of actually eating with us. The good silverware gleamed on the red and white embroidered tablecloth, the polished crystal water and wine glasses positioned just so, our best plates with their gold rims and green filigree border warmed and shining, the matching platters and bowls filled with hot food, ornate serving spoons placed alongside: we were finally ready to eat. My father poured me a small glass of red wine and we started with a toast to one another, to Mops, to Santa, and to my mother's father, my Opa. I secretly toasted Oma, too: she was my favourite.

As we ate, compliments cascading upon my mother who pretended not to notice, I couldn't take my eyes off our Christmas tree, a white spruce festooned with a silvery gold garland that had been carefully lifted out of its cardboard box and draped with precision in elegant and ever-widening swoops around the circumference—"Pull it down further on the left, Keith: it's not matching what you did on the right"—and several strands of round, frosted electric lights, red, green, yellow, blue, reflecting on a thousand glittered glass ornaments, many of them family treasures, hand-painted and intricate—"You've got two the same side by side, Keith: move the one on your right." Tinsel icicles completed the effect, artfully placed to fill gaps and accentuate the decorations. Family lore had it that on my parents' first Christmas together, my father followed his own tradition of flinging the tinsel haphazardly onto the tree, like spaghetti onto a wall, letting it stay wherever it landed. "Keith!" I could hear my mother shriek. "Are you mad?" I was not allowed to place the tinsel: after going to school on it, that was my father's job.

Convinced we had the most beautiful tree in the neighbourhood, I brought school chums home to admire it, standing back to watch their faces, counting the seconds until they could breathe again and turn to me to proclaim, "Oh, I wish we had a tree like that!" Did anyone ever actually say that? I don't remember. My love for our tree and its green

aroma was enough. I waited for the harsh afternoon sun to go down so it could transform itself into a dazzling confection against the backdrop of the dark.

After dinner, I helped with the dishes—probably the only time when I didn't rebel at a task I hated, finding skills that eluded me the rest of the year: suddenly I could dry those dishes fast enough, perfectly enough, and anticipate instructions, replacing the dish towel unbidden when it became wet, reaching to put things away rather than leaving them on the counter, offering to do the extras. And then, finally, rewarded for my patience, it was time for Christmas.

I put three glossy, lemon-iced lebkuchen on a plate, admittedly with some reluctance as I cherished those spicy cookies for myself, and set them on the kitchen table along with the requisite glass of milk, where Santa couldn't fail to see them. Then my mother, Mops and I made our annual pilgrimage down the hall to my bedroom at the back of the house, where we waited for Santa Claus to come, hoping that he wouldn't be frightened, trusting in my father to have just the right way of chatting him up, inviting him in, encouraging him to drop his boulder-sized sack and find within it all the packages addressed to me, the child of this house, the one who adored and believed. It was enough that Santa would have to grapple with a house that didn't have a chimney, requiring his reindeer to land on an unadorned roof, and he himself having somehow to reach the ground, I suspected by way of the drain pipe, which I would inspect the morning after for lost buttons—and so given these unfortunate challenges, we could not allow him to experience any additional frustrations.

That was why my mother, Mops and I waited in that back bedroom, aware that Santa didn't like to be looked at in his work, and why my mother exhorted me to stay away from the windows, those windows so black, so full of portent, like the next page of my storybook that couldn't come fast enough when my babysitter lingered too long with the turning. I couldn't take my eyes off them. "Shh," my mother said, and Mops responded to the tension, his silly ears on high alert, one up, one sideways, his stubby tail wagging questioningly as he searched our faces, looked toward the bedroom door, listened to my father go back and forth down the hall as he transferred gifts from my parents' bedroom to the Christmas tree. At least I had that little ritual figured out. I counted those trips, relishing each additional one he made, willing him to go on.

And then silence. A thud, and silence again. And then the doorbell. The doorbell! Where on earth was Daddy, why was he not standing vigil by the door...and I would have to throw my body on top of Mops, creating a human tent with my elbows and knees to contain his frenzy, to muffle his frantic barks and prevent him from scaring Santa away, my bottom in the air, my heart hammering, Mops's heart hammering, my hand around his muzzle as he squirmed, whispering to him, "It's okay Mops, it's okay Mops," and then muffled talking in the front hall, and silence again and me not daring to let the dog go and then the front door opening and again more talking, and silence. Silence, crackling.

My mother looked at me, her eyes wide, and I looked at her, mine wider, and we both mouthed "Shh" to each other, holding our fingers to our lips as we waited for the cue, and then it came: the sound of our little white ceramic bell that sat on the buffet, the precious heirloom I was not allowed to touch, its silvery tinkling my father's signal that it was time for the three of us to join him in the living room. And we filed out of the bedroom, Mops first, and down the darkened hall, which had somehow stretched in length to the span of our street, if not the 401, and into a festival of dancing lights.

My father had lit a dozen sparklers on the tree, and the spectacle of them as we rounded the corner, foaming and frothing, the room ablaze in a confetti of light, brightly coloured parcels and ribbon tumbling out from under the tree like molten gold from a magic spring, sent my hand to my mouth to suppress an inarticulate "Oh!" As we approached, he carefully placed the needle in the proper groove on the vinyl record for that old familiar melody, *Stille Nacht, Helige Nacht*, and we joined him by the tree and stood there, arms around each other, swaying and singing in German the achingly familiar refrain of that beautiful carol, followed by *O Tannenbaum*, countless points of light from the tree reflecting in our eyes, Mops scoping out the gifts, everything in order, peace and harmony like a warm shawl around my shoulders, our only religion in that sweet, short, sanctified time of my life: family and trust. And it was enough.

After the singing, my father removed the sparklers, now fizzled to red embers, and turned up the lights to a romantic level, while I gazed lovingly at the small pile of gifts set apart from the rest, a little snow still melting on them, knowing they were from Santa. Next I checked the kitchen table, noting with mixed emotion that this year he had eaten all three cookies, the spilled crumbs attesting to his enjoyment, the glass of milk drained. I marveled at him, making his countless stops through the night, arriving in the homes of other European families the world over in the nick of time, pulling out labeled presents from his sack, his pleasure increasing as his load lightened, and I wondered at his capacity to eat all the cookies his children left him. How I loved that portly man and his belly, his endearing fear of being seen, his big generous heart.

Especially his big generous heart, especially where it concerned me.

Our Christmas lasted late into the night, my father in his red vest sitting on a stuffed stool by the tree, leisurely handing out gifts, one at a time, all of us oohing and ahhing over the other's prize, especially over those packages whose extravagance in wrapping outshone the contents, laughing at the sometimes cheeky, sometimes mysterious messages my mother liked to write on the tags, trying on new clothes, creating a mountain of wrapping paper in the middle of the room for Mops to hide in, laughing at his one brown eye peering through the heap at us, laughing at each other, my father clowning, my mother liking it, and everything was good. My father took frequent breaks to change the music and fix us drinks, my mother, master-weaver of this family romance, looked beautiful, her chestnut hair held up with a diamond comb, her lips red, her mood expansive, and we stretched out time, performing our ceremonies in the holy space we'd created together until close to midnight, an unimaginable privilege for a little girl normally required to observe strict bedtimes.

Finally installed once again in my bedroom, my parents gone to theirs, and the Christmas tree dark, I had the freedom at last to approach the window, able at last to peer out without risk, and wait for my best friend Jennifer to leave with her family for midnight mass at the Catholic school-turned-church behind our house. I watched their shadowy shapes walk down their driveway across the street, and flashed my Aladdin's lamp at her, our secret signal of solidarity: "all is well." This done, I turned to my bed.

And even then it wasn't over. My father, determined to inject into our Christmas tradition a ritual from his own family practices, left me a stocking to open in the morning, full of small cherished gifts like coloured pens and pencils, a sharpener, some sweets, perhaps a Dinky toy, a yellow tractor: my passion. Two more packages waited for me: the white-cloth one from my father's mother, my grandma, sent overseas from England, the seams sewn with heavy thread in big stitches with her own hand, and the second one wrapped in brown paper and taped so determinedly as to be a virtual fortress, resistant to scissors, from his sister, my beloved Auntie Winn, also from England.

It was a second Christmas I was content to celebrate by myself, blissful in its way, my parents never able to rouse themselves on weekend and holiday mornings, especially Christmas Day.

After the final unwrapping, I feasted on lebkuchen, for surely I would be forgiven any pilfering from the verboten stash of cookies on this one special day, rummaged through my gifts, tried on the new fuzzy slippers, modelled my new pink flannelette nightie in the hallway mirror, and best of all, fondled my ten new books, pressing them against my nose to smell the paper and ink, stacking them by author, then by size, teasing myself with a first page there, two pages here, finally settling on the couch with the chosen story, oblivious to the slow advance of the morning, until Daddy, rising around noon, made us fried eggs, sunny side up, on toast.

Christmas.

Christmas: a word so round and spilling over with light, colour and music, so linked with love and replete with contentment, that it lives in my mind like a person. I still savour it, feel the smack of it, thrill to it, follow its million tiny electrical impulses to the places in my child's body where the memories seat themselves.

Santa took my name off his list decades ago. Even so, that old familiar love affair wells up inside me on schedule, reaching its zenith each December 24: a legacy from my family, small in number, large of heart.

The Snow Plough

By Carole Payne

The trouble was that his stories were always compelling. He needed money for this or that urgent thing and you believed him and gladly handed it over to help him out. The magic worked until you were burned and got angry with him and then he moved on. He was always making big promises, new beginnings. His earnestness about the next scheme caught you every time. He knew you wanted to believe him and he was a master at plucking your heartstrings. It seemed it was his only gift.

But he always blew it. He avoided certain people because he owed them money. He stayed away from certain bars where he had caused trouble. And he couldn't go back to that small town restaurant where he had scammed a meal with the promise of bringing a group of guys from his union for a huge party. He smiles when he remembers how he had talked the waitress into giving him a fabulous meal, and three kinds of beer on tap because he needed to make sure the boys only got the best. It had all gone well until she came out to the car to say goodbye and saw the half dozen cell phones on the seat and called her friend, the local cop who ran the license plate on the stolen car and he had been busted again.

In spite of driving her and their teenage son crazy, he and his wife are still together. In the last year someone has lent him money to set up a business in a store front with his promise that when it takes off the lender will get his investment back in spades. He leaves the house every day to go to his business, shaved and dressed in a suit and tie. But he does not go there because he doesn't know anything about business, can't handle money. He owes rent and hasn't paid anything for the machinery that sits gleaming and unused at the back of the store. The bailiff came last week and padlocked the door, but he hasn't yet told his wife. He has gone, instead, as is his custom, to the bar, this time with the last of the money from the loan.

This night he drinks until he is very drunk and the bartender closes the bar. At three o'clock in the morning, he staggers home, lets himself into the house, ready to pass out. Just his luck, his wife is waiting for him in the kitchen.

The predictable arguments begin, except they are worse because she has had a visit from the bailiff and her rage is honed from waiting for him. It is too familiar. His promises, his failures, his drinking, and his using up the money they need for food. He is a loser beyond losers. The shouting gets louder. There are threats of violence. He is a big man and he looms over her in his suit and tie and greatcoat. A drunk.

He hears his son's voice, low, urgent, and moves quickly to the hall table to stop the call. He rips the telephone out of the wall and throws it at him. Damn the boy. He will kill the young bastard yet.

Fearing that the police will book him, he staggers out into the cold before they get there. He stumbles around the streets of St. Catharines for hours, trying to sort out his options. He knows the cops will tell his wife to get a restraining order to keep him away from the house and he knows this time his wife will do it. He will be thrown out. He will have no place to stay. He can't tolerate the thought of actually hitting his wife or his boy, but he is so low, he no longer trusts himself. He will start again. He will show them that he really can do it. He will make it somewhere else.

At the bus station, he makes up a story about needing to see his sick mother in St. Joe's in Toronto and shamelessly takes money from the frail, white-haired lady who smiles sympathetically at him as she hands over forty dollars. He boards the bus to Toronto, sitting at the back, dully watching people get on and off. The bus ride seems interminable. He hates sitting still but he worries that if he causes any trouble, the driver will throw him off.

He has not been to the city for a long time, but he knows it well enough to worry that someone might remember him at the Good Shepherd or the Victor. He remembers that The Salvation Army is not an option either. The last time he was at the Army, he had been banned for life for trashing the place after a particularly bad bender. That leaves the Scott Mission. He is starving and aching for a drink. The lady at the Scott eyes him but doesn't question him. Nothing surprises her anymore. Guys of all kinds show up at the Scott when there are no options left. She gives him a chit to get some food and accepts what he says about being homeless.

He scarfs down the soup and sandwiches and keeps to himself. He sleeps fitfully, if at all. This is not the worst shelter he has been in, but it has the usual contingent of half-crazy guys who shout out in their sleep. He worries about the frightened young kid in the corner, who probably has a knife in his shoe. He has nothing worth stealing, but he is still wearing the suit and tie, not having had the time to take a change of clothes when he said goodbye to his life.

He leaves in the middle of the night, has to sign out, usual crap. He has no money, no plan, feeling hungover and now, pissed, angry at his wife, at his kid who called the cops, and who looks too much like the kid with the knife in the corner, scared. He is certainly pissed at the cops. He walks east, taking back alleys and avoiding the main streets. He tries to avoid stumbling over men who are homeless like him but who are too proud or too scared to use the shelters. They are bundled up in sleeping bags over heating grates, the soft snow covering them, melting, covering them again. Prostitutes on street corners in bare legs and high heels, seeing his suit and presuming he has a warm room, call out to him, but he looks angry and they are not disappointed when he ignores them.

The heat from the alcohol is wearing off quickly and the cold is seeping into his bones. His is suddenly aware that he is forty-four years old and he doesn't have a plan for his life.

He passes the City's Eastern Works Yard. The salting and sanding trucks are already out, keeping the streets passable. The snow is falling steadily now. His mood suddenly lightens at the sight of the big snowploughs being warmed up. He knows how to drive one of those suckers. Well, he hasn't actually driven a snowplough, but before he was stuck with the store front, he had taken that operating heavy machinery course at the community college in Niagara Falls, and although idiot boy in short pants hadn't let him have his certificate until he had "a better attitude," he *had* driven an eighteen-wheeler and learned to back it up. He was pretty good on a forklift, too.

A light goes on in his head. He walks through the yard gate. Friggin' supervisor takes one look at his size and then at his suit. He shakes his head when he tells him he has experience and asks if he can get a morning's work.

"This is a union job, Mac." He shakes his head and turns away.

"Sure, man."

He walks away, with the only idea since he left St. Catharines in the toilet. Out of the corner of his eye he sees a maintenance guy hop out of one of the big suckers that he has just started. He smiles. He can pick himself up after all. He is tired of this friggin' weather. He is tired of everything. He needs wheels. He slips, unnoticed into the cab of the big machine, slides the snowplough into gear. Staring straight ahead he heads out into the wide, white world of Toronto's morning traffic. The cab window is shut tight so he doesn't

hear the frantic shouting behind him.
    New beginnings. The sun is just coming up and the sky is shining with a bright winter light. He will show them. He will show them all...

Cacotopia

By Michael Hanlon

Everyone hereabouts agrees that our mayor, Ed Bouchard, is the best-dressed man in town. It's no great surprise, really. His son Fraser owns 11 Savile Row, Cacotopia's only up-scale men's clothing store, and Mayor Eddie, as we all call him, gets a forty-five per cent discount. Besides, we have few up-scale men to clothe, most being decidedly down-market and given to beer-brand T-shirts or a style best described as Walmart Hawaiian. So something from 11 Savile Row would make even a troll stand out.

And, as Jillian Proctor, the mayor's hoity-toity English secretary, puts it, Eddie does cut something of a dash. Even astride his bike, one foot on the curb for balance as he waits for the lights to change and his head domed by a safety helmet, Mayor Eddie looks the part, groomed to a shine, a well put-together, natty five-foot four.

"Ever wonder, Mayor Eddie, who sets the sequences for these lights?" I asked as I prepared to saunter across to the Arnold Spleen Branch of Cacotopia Public Library.

"Damned if I know," he said, shooting a cuff to glance at his Breitling, obtained through a deal with Councillor Orland Pearson of Pearson's Jewellery & Gifts. "Seems like I've been here an hour or more, and there's another sequence to go before I get a green."

Cacotopia, Caco to its citizens, has even more traffic lights than it has tattoo parlours and nail salons. This surfeit comes up regularly at the Star Chamber, the table at Duffy's where the town's geezers gather of a morning to tear apart the Caco Daily Star and settle all our problems.

"Like we could start a new book club, call it the Red Light Club," intoned the Reverend Ephraim Foster as he dunked something labeled a biscotti in his mug of tea with milk, two sugars. "You could read a couple chapters waiting for green. I'm halfway through *War and Peace* since Tuesday last."

Tommy "Pit Stop" Perkins, former chief mechanic at Hobbs's Motors (Councillor Selwyn Archbold, prop.), nudged Pastor Foster. "If you don't mind my saying so, Reverend," he whispered, "I think you're supposed to do that with coffee."

"You're crazy," Pastor Foster said. "I can't read *War and Peace*, keep an eye on the light AND drink coffee all at the same time."

Mornings are like that at the Star Chamber at Duffy's.

Caco's female opinion-moulders gather at the Milk Maid, a name left over from its days as a strip joint where the ladies dressed as milk maids and carried milking stools they used for table-dancing. Business was pretty good until Madison Plumstead teetered off her stool in mid-performance one evening and knocked over her sister Valerie, the other dancer, who was working the adjacent table, causing her to break her ankle.

To the consternation of Bernie Plumstead, the girls' father and owner of the Milk Maid, the bartender called for an ambulance and as its siren grew nearer, the patrons exited in haste and never came back.

So the Milk Maid Café (formerly Lounge) is doing nicely, what with the regular coffee ladies after the breakfast rush, the Red Hat Ladies lunching every two weeks and the Word Witches first and third Fridays.

"I'm concerned about Mayor Eddie," said Sabine Sprott, whose husband Steve owns almost everything in Caco bar 11 Savile Row, Pearson's Jewellery and Gifts, Hobbs's Motors, Duffy's and the Milk Maid (Valerie Plumstead now owns the

Milk Maid). Sabine's companions leaned forward, minds eagerly open for a new rumour, spice, gossip, anything.

"It's about the roundabouts," Sabine said. The ladies slumped back in their chairs, hopes expunged.

"What about the roundabouts?" Helen Varley asked. "They're not going to be round enough for you?"

Sabine leaned forward herself, hastily glancing over each shoulder as though fearing eavesdroppers.

"They're being sabotaged," she said. "Some people – I won't say who here – are trying to sabotage the roundabouts, Mayor Eddie's number one project right now. He needs them after the failure of the pool project in Queen Mum Park."

She sat back, waiting for a shocked response.

"Emma's pig is coming home," Ethel Ostrand said. "It's been four years now and today's only Tuesday." Actually, today was Thursday. Ethel was having an Ethel moment.

"Sabotage, you say," said Elsie Chessnut, widow of former mayor Cedric Chessnut. "And how do you come by this secret intelligence, Sabine? Tell us that."

"Well," said Sabine, who not only talked like Ronald Reagan but looked somewhat like him, what with her tan and her orange hair. "Well... my grandson Nathan (Oh Christ, muttered Susie Planck, not her grandson Nathan again) has been working on a project in his computer class at North CI and so he looked in some emails being sent between people in the Traffic Light Division at Public Works."

"Wait a minute," said Doc Fox, who used to be chief orthopedic surgeon at the old hospital until it got replaced by the new medical theme park "Health by the Plateful," proclaim the ads for its open-to-the-public Hale 'n' Hearty Cafeteria. "Isn't reading other people's emails illegal? It's called hi-jacking or something."

"My heavens, no," said Sabine. "Nathan would never do anything illegal."

"Like his grandfather, eh?" Elsie said.

"Sabine's off on one of her crusades again," Steve Sprott said. "She's got a bee up her ass about the roundabouts."

"It's a bee in her bonnet," Pit Stop said. "She's got a bee in her bonnet."

"No," Sprott said. "Other people get a bee in their bonnet. Sabine gets a bee up her ass."

"Anyway, those roundabouts are a pain in the ass, you ask me," Pit Stop commented. "Just because we're getting a new...what is it? 'Cultural Hub for Cacotopia'...don't mean we have to have them European things in the middle of the road. They're against nature. Our cars can't handle 'em."

Sprott took a sip of his white wine spritzer, all he could handle at The Duck & Drake since his last check-up. "It's not Sabine or the roundabouts I'm worried about," he said. "This time she's got Nathan involved."

Nathan was loving it. Grandma thought he was a genius. Ashley Baines, the babe next door and the only person other than Grandma who knew what he was doing, thought he was cool. Grandpa, he thought, knew there was something going on and that he was being kept out of it. Which was fine with Nathan. He loved Grandpa dearly but Grandpa had a finger in everything in Capo and Nathan, like Grandpa, liked being on the inside. He felt like a secret agent. Shit, he said to himself, I am a secret agent.

By chance, while roaming the web looking for help on an assignment about civic government, he'd found himself staring at emails that obviously were about Caco's roundabouts. Dull stuff, he thought. But as he was about to hit delete, the word "sabotage" leapt off the screen.

The subject was Project Circles. It was from a Clive Cranston to a Geoff Dinham. "We can't let this go ahead," it said. "Our very existence is at stake. We must find some way to stop it. Once they let those in the town, there'll be nothing but roundabouts. I'm not suggesting sabotage, of course, but nothing can stand in our way. Don't show this msg to anyone."

Nathan printed it out and closed it. And then he wished he could remember how he'd found access to it. A smart kid of fourteen, it took him all of eight minutes to find his way back in. He found more emails, all on the same subject, all between Cranston and Dinham. No one else seemed involved.

It wasn't until he was over at Grandpa and Grandma's the next evening and heard them discussing the roundabouts that Nathan realised he'd gone platinum. Back home, he opened his laptop and went to the Caco Municipality website. Cranston, he found, was the Director of Public Works. Dinham was Supervisor of Traffic Light Strategy.

"So how's high school coming along?" Grandma asked next day as she gave him a Coke and ten bucks for cutting the grass. "What's your favourite subject?"

"Computer science, I guess," Nathan replied.

"I don't understand any of it," Grandma said. "It's all Latvian to me."

"Greek, Grandma," Nathan said. "All Greek. There's lots of neat stuff."

"Like what?"

Nathan, hoping he could score another Coke and perhaps an increase in the mowing rate, shared a little of his secret.

"Oh, my Lord," Grandma said. "This is serious. Don't tell Grandpa."

"Okay," Nathan said.

"Don't tell anyone. Particularly don't tell your teacher."

While hearing his father cursing Caco traffic lights on their way home from soccer that evening, Nathan decided that he'd search Dinham's computer. Much of it was dull but the section on *Sequencing at Major Intersections – Thought Experiment* had him glued to the screen.

Wait-times between reds and greens were being

changed sometimes three times a day, all at Dinham's whim. The five-way intersection by the Holiday Inn would sometimes have right turns on red going east and west, an hour later going north and south. Wait-times were extended so that as many as twenty cars in a row were backed up, only to be given a green that sent a flood of vehicles out filling the road ahead so that no waiting vehicles could cross it.

At Central Mall, where three sets of lights were staggered with reds and greens appearing within five yards of each other, Dinham had set up a CCTV so that he could sit in his office and watch the drivers' confusion.

Nathan was no driver but he'd heard his father, and his mother, even his grandma, rant about the traffic sequences every time they went for a ride. He saw an heroic role ahead for himself. He would hack into Dinham's website and fix the system.

"Gosh darn it, Nathan," Grandpa said as the facing lane got an advanced green while he sat and fumed, "why doesn't someone do something about this town's traffic lights?"

"Maybe no one knows how," Nathan said with a sly smile.

The next morning, while Grandpa settled himself for a long wait by the Holiday Inn, the light went green within ten seconds. He was third in line so he didn't make it across before the light changed again. But, by golly, ten seconds later, he was on his way.

Same when he and Grandma cruised up to the lights at Central Mall that afternoon. Five lights, no waiting.

Service vehicles were racing out of Public Works to near every intersection in Caco – there were only two that didn't have lights – and Dinham sat at his computer changing each one individually back to three- and four-minute sequencing. But as soon as he got home from school, Nathan changed them back to ten seconds.

Drivers didn't like ten seconds much, either, but

Nathan was on a mission. Somehow he'd become politicized and adept at intrigue. His own sabotage, he realised, could prevent theirs. What they needed was an ultimatum.

He knew better than to deliver it by email. That could soon be traced. But he'd learned Morse code in the Scouts and now he decided to use it. It took him about two hours to complete the programming but by bed-time it was ready to be installed.

As soon as he woke, he called Dinham's home number, easily found in the Caco book, and, after putting a face cloth over the mouthpiece, told Dinham to go to the Holiday Inn intersection at noon and watch the lights.

"And take someone with you who can read Morse," his heavy, growly voice ordered.

Dinham called the local Coast Guard station and at noon, he was at the Holiday Inn. "I don't get it," the Coast Guard officer said. "'Leave the roundabouts alone and you can have your lights back'. What the hell is that supposed to mean?"

Two months later, Nathan went with Grandpa and Grandma to watch the official opening of the roundabouts at the Cultural Hub.

Mayor Eddie was the first to navigate the circles. On his bike. Looking natty as ever.

That afternoon, Ashley Baines gave Nathan his first real kiss.

The Bone Doctor and the Undercover Patient

By Lori Pearson

I thought we must be watching an episode of Oprah when Daffy entered the ward. "Body dysmorphic disorder," I proclaimed sagely. Apparently no one else remembered that episode of Oprah. The rest couldn't believe what they were seeing.

Daffy was an artificial blonde with big tits and Ubangi lips. I don't mean to be unkind but she was Barbie on steroids. Her personality matched her appearance. She always seemed to have a cell phone in hand and always seemed to be talking very loudly about her Porsche on the phone. No one really believed she was talking to anybody. She never had visitors. Very oddly, her only friend on the ward was a born again Christian, who wore long shapeless dresses, devoutly attended ECT three times a week and on the surface seemed to be the opposite of every trait that Daffy possessed.

The Daffy problem seemed to go on for weeks. We all appeared to like and accept Daffy while in therapy sessions, but when we gathered at the smoke shack to try to make sense of our world, she became Daffy — so named because of the protruding lips that made her resemble a duck. We discussed her each and every imagined social transgression, pointedly moved away from her when she started one of her loud, rambling Porsche phone calls. It all came to a head when she developed a crush on Malkie.

We called him Malkie because of his uncanny resemblance to the actor John Malkovich. The resemblance was purely physical. Malkie spent a lot of time lying in bed in a darkened room and when he ventured out, he was mouse-like quiet, making himself appear very small. He did not like to be noticed. However, Daffy found him suitable prey.

She wandered into the commissary and purchased a bottle of aftershave for Malkie. It was a strangely personal and yet inappropriate gift. Malkie rarely had it in him to shave and he had no stomach for getting himself involved with the ladies. In panic, he fled to the smoke shack to ask us what he should do.

It was an afternoon to remember. We all took turns embellishing the potential for this romantic entanglement. With each story, Malkie's prowess became more legendary, the imagined coupling of Malkie and Daffy becoming more colourful as we each took a stab at describing the possibilities. Malkie, strangely enough, seemed to get off on these tales, his usual foggy expression morphing into delight. We were amazed at the transformative grin which only increased our attempts to really bring the story home. We were laughing till tears ran down our faces with each imagined position; each imagined result – the possibility of this gift of aftershave becoming a springboard for Malkie who would now possess unlimited virility and imagination, not to mention desirability and attractiveness.

Someone determined that Malkie should henceforth be known as "The Bone Doctor" as he now possessed a cure for the ladies, albeit imaginary.

This joke temporarily laid to rest; the conversation digressed to the mundane. It was a recurring agenda item at these meetings to discuss the case, perhaps a myth, of the undercover patient.

In these wards, there walked, we were sure, a psychiatrist masquerading as a patient. An enemy among us, listening in at the smoke shack, the dining room, group therapy, bowling – all the places we might be momentarily off guard. It was in line with our belief that we had all become ill due to experimentation by a large drug company – no matter what label we wore as individuals, we all took the same drugs to try to control our illnesses. There is no cure, you see, when you are diagnosed with a mental illness. It is all about control.

We looked to each other with beady, suspicious eyes, perhaps the only hope being for us as individuals that one of us was the undercover patient and the drugs had made us forget who we truly were. At some point, experiment over, drugs withdrawn, a return to normal.

Later that night, we saw Malkie and Daffy holding hands. There were no jokes, just a sadness that they had found a way to connect despite us. With an unspoken consensus, Daffy and the Bone Doctor ceased to exist in the smoke shack while the undercover patient's reports became a mystery to be unearthed, the lies that he or she was reporting.

It was patently clear to all of us that the undercover patient was the only reason that we were all still here.

A Canadian Winter's Tale

By Margaret Bain

Decades ago, in a period of joblessness and austerity not dissimilar to the present, we left London, England, for Ontario. We rented a small apartment, which seemed pleasantly spacious, as we waited, for several months, for our furniture to arrive. When the freighter carrying our household goods had finished exploring the world's oceans at its leisure, our modest collection of tables and chairs and boxes of books and other paraphernalia was finally delivered, and suddenly our small apartment looked just that – small.

So it seemed a good time to start looking at houses. We were city souls, used to a big metropolis, and of course completely unused to Canadian winters. But we were seized with the thought that it might be fun to live in the country instead of the town, perhaps in one of those lovely farmhouses we had admired along the back roads, built by 19th-century Scottish stonemasons, we were told.

By this time it was winter, and it was snowing a lot. One afternoon we set out in our dark green Beaumont, which sashayed about the road at the best of times, and wandered scenic rural byways as a few fat snowflakes fell lazily from the low grey sky. A perfect stone farmhouse surrounded by a small grove of trees appeared to our right, up a long snow-covered driveway, a For Sale sign half obscured in a roadside snowdrift. My husband swung the wheel a trifle abruptly towards the driveway, and my side of the car suddenly dropped at a very odd angle. "Maggie, do hop out and see what's happened," he said. Obediently, I opened the passenger door, and my shiny, white, knee-high Mary Quant boots made a perfect entry point, worthy of an Olympic diver, into the deep, snow-filled ditch.

I was very pregnant and, alas, even heavier than I should have been, as my kindly obstetrician had noted with many a regretful sigh, so I plummeted down through the soft, fluffy snow effortlessly until my toes touched bottom, and I stopped, with snow right up to my chin. With much huffing and puffing, I was extricated from my plight, but there we were, long before the time of cell-phones, our car in a ditch on a lightly-travelled road, with no really warm clothes or survival gear, and it was getting dark.

We hardly had time to feel as panic-stricken as we deserved. The next three cars coming along the road all stopped. The first driver jumped out and produced a tow rope, the second and third helped him attach it to the Beaumont, and as we watched, totally amazed, these three complete strangers, without a word to each other or to us, hoisted our car out of the ditch, re-stowed tow ropes and hitches, and drove off, as we tried to stammer out heartfelt thanks.

My goodness, we thought, Canada must be a wonderful country. And of course it is.

Life, Death and Resurrection

By Mary Fleming

We needed a family pet, four children really, really needed a pet; alas their father was not quite so keen. He had enough mouths to feed already, anyway he had grown up on a farm and didn't want to see any more four-legged creatures looking up at him with sad, searching, hungry eyes. I was happy enough so long as the care and cleaning didn't fall to mother and they promised it wouldn't. Hmm, now what kind of pet would keep everyone happy? And so the arguments began...

The girls definitely favoured a cat. I vetoed that one: too smelly; birds were mentioned, but what can you do with a bird, and they are messy. Goldfish, well now they did not seem to live very long here. We had already killed off (with kindness of course) a sizeable number of their population. Finally, a dog passed all the tests, especially with the boys who were already seeing Rover fetching balls, scaring the mailman and generally running havoc in the neighbourhood; it was a macho thing. They assured their father they would teach Rover to fetch his slippers every night when he came home – and he believed them!

What kind of dog would keep everyone happy? We seemed to have lots of choice, so the sensible thing to do was to visit a kennel and see if love at first sight hit anyone. Well something did hit but it sure was not love – we were about two minutes inside the barn door and Christy started to wheeze, sneeze and itch. *Ah!* I thought (and I could not help smiling) *Christy is allergic to dogs* – he already had every other allergy so dogs were a sure bet for inclusion. The children were disappointed but understanding of their sibling's medical crisis, we left for home sans dog.

We were just inside the door when Lesley insisted we hadn't really solved our problem. The others looked at her and in her own sweet, take-charge way, she thought it would be a lovely idea if we got a turtle. That caused a few laughs, of course. "What are you going to do with it – make soup? What can a turtle do? Jump fences?"

Lesley ignored them all as she usually did and said she would buy it herself out of her very own pocket money – and she did, well almost. Tommy came home, settled in, and learned a few tricks, so they told me, like looking up and begging? Racing on the floor? He really aced hiding behind a large rock in his bowl. Indeed, one of God's most talented creatures — weren't we lucky!

We grew to love the little fellow until one morning I came downstairs to great wails. Tommy was dead! He had already been prodded, poked, shaken – all the usual medical tests but alas, he remained quite inert. Yes, I had to conclude — Tommy was definitely dead. I figured the garbage bucket, a clean out of the bowl and another of his clan could move in but a horrified Lesley told me, no! We had to give Tommy a proper Christian burial, interred into a proper grave, with a service that she herself would arrange and lead, of course. And we all had to attend. Her sister suddenly remembered she had to meet a friend so off she disappeared. The boys, in gruesome glee got into the act and once they had decided on the location, under a tree of course, all the best graves are under trees — started digging. I wondered if they intended sending Tommy to Australia and had to go out and tell them three inches was quite deep enough. Lesley felt she did not want any container and a sleep in the cool earth was just so right for her best friend. I felt I might never be able to keep a straight face so after fortifying myself with a good strong coffee, went out to the service. I even took off my apron and washed my hands – It was a formal affair. We sang a hymn. No, I don't remember which one; I don't think they knew too many hymns at that age — and into the ground went Tommy.

The rest of the day was sad; we talked about our missing friend, told father what he had missed by going to work and finally, night fell and everyone went off to bed. Tomorrow was another day, praises be!

It was a bright sunny, warm day and first thing Lesley did when she came down was rush out to visit her friend's grave, having decided to lay a few flowers, freshly picked from my rose garden, on his plot. Off she went and a few minutes later, we all heard her cries. "He's alive, he's alive."

The entire family rushed out to see this miracle and there on the ground, looking up at us in complete bewilderment sat Tommy, seemingly none the worse for his interment.

I could say it was a happy-ever-after time but I seem to remember that Tommy did actually die – and stay dead – only a few weeks later and of course there was another service, although not quite so dramatic as his first burial, but certainly every bit as sincere.

The end? – oh no, years later Lesley became a minister, conducting many a funeral, although none quite so moving and dramatic as her first venture and often at Easter when the children are learning about the resurrection she tells them the story of good old Tommy and how he lived, died and rose again.

So much easier for little minds to understand.
AMEN

Freedom 55

By Ann Partridge

Shelly sighed deeply, in relief she was quite sure. It was done. Her working life was at an end. She hadn't voluntarily retired, but being made redundant in her mid-fifties qualified as the finish line. Her imagination didn't stretch to doing up a resumé and hunting for a new position after all these years. With her severance package and pension she would be all right. Wouldn't she?

No more dealing with clueless clients and absorbing their frustration at the incomprehensible ways of government grants. She would miss the everyday chatter of a few co-workers, but not the backstabbing digs of many of the others. She was free from all that now. Freedom 55. That thought caused her to give a sharp bark of nervous laughter.

She celebrated her newfound freedom by making a whole pot of coffee instead of her customary single cup. Adjusting her velour bathrobe, she savoured the freshly-ground coffee and allowed herself one more sigh as she studied the angle of sunlight on her back deck. She had rarely taken the time to examine her surroundings, she realized.

During her working years she had always had a schedule. It revolved around work during the week and then Saturday was her day to resupply groceries, clothes, home cleaning and maintenance supplies. Sundays she cleaned her townhouse from top to bottom, did laundry and arranged meals and everything so she was well organized for her work week. No sitting around contemplating her life. At least not since Frank left and before that...she refused to go there on her first day of...she would call it retirement, rather than unemployment.

Pouring herself another cup of coffee, she noticed the sun now shining directly through her sliding glass doors and onto the floor. Shedding her memory-foam slippers, she sat down, leaned back and extended her feet into the pool of warmth. Maybe she could spring for a pedicure this week, she thought. Or, should she conserve her funds and forego treats like that? It's not like anyone ever saw her feet. But she did and she would appreciate the bit of pampering, she decided.

Now what? The thought shattered her sunlit reflections.

Her heart started to pound. Jamming her feet back into her slippers, Shelly tucked her legs under her chair. She held her ceramic coffee mug with two hands and huddled over its warmth. Why hadn't she made plans for this day? And all the days stretching ahead of her. Had she been in denial?

Thinking back, she could see that she had refused to acknowledge, even to herself, that her life revolved around work. The office had become her haven. When her home life had spiralled out of her control, work had become her touchstone. Things were routine there. There were rules and regulations governing her conduct and that of those around her and she was well able to operate under those conditions. There weren't any surprises she didn't feel capable of dealing with at work.

The office atmosphere was a direct contrast to the emotion-fraught family relationships that had torn her apart and left her desolate.

Now she was feeling the same way about her no-longer-necessary job. Shelly felt abandoned once again and this time she had no safe haven. Now when she looked at the sunlight streaming into her kitchen, what caught her eye were the streaks on the glass doors and the dust coating the floor. When her next sip of coffee proved cold, her head fell forward.

Finally, fighting inertia, she pushed herself into a standing position with a groan. This brought to mind something someone had once said: that a sign of old age was when you groaned at every small effort. Shaking her head at her rapid downward mood spiral, she poured her cold coffee down the sink and looked at the half-full pot. She might as well try another cup. Or, should she get dressed first? Why bother? As she was pouring coffee into her mug, she remembered the bottle of Bailey's one of her co-workers had given her as a leaving gift. With a fatalistic shrug, she found the bottle in the cupboard, opened it and poured a few inches into her coffee. She could use something to spark some enthusiasm for her new life. It was unlikely she would fall under the spell of the demon alcohol with just the one bottle of Irish cream. Right?

As she lifted the mug to her mouth, her phone rang. She set the coffee down quickly, as if she had been caught out. Shaking her head at her misplaced guilt, she checked the caller ID. Work. Well, what do you know? Maybe they can't manage without her, either.

Oddly enough, it was Gilda, the woman who had presented her with the Bailey's. "Hey, Shelly, how do you like being a woman of leisure?"

"It will take some getting used to, but so far so good. What's up?"

"Kendra, from Social Services called for you. I offered to take the information and told her that you weren't here any-more. She asked if you could give her a call, so I said I would relay the information. Do you want her number?"

"Sure," Shelly said.

Gilda read out the number and then made vague suggestions for a future lunch. Shelly went along with the polite charade, thanked her and hung up.

Looking at the phone number she had written down, she tried to guess what Kendra wanted. They had shared information from time to time when researching clients and had developed a comfortable working relationship. Ideally, a job opportunity would be the best case scenario, but Shelly didn't really think that was likely. She couldn't think of any unfinished business between them. Maybe Kendra just wanted to wish her well in the future.

Shelly sipped her coffee, smiled in surprise at the sweet goodness of the Bailey's and dialled the number. She didn't actually reach Kendra: her call was routed to a receptionist who informed her that Kendra had an opening at 1:30 that afternoon, if Shelly could come down to the Social Services building to meet with her.

Shelly frowned, hesitated for a moment and then agreed to the meeting. It would give her something to do today, even if she was unsure what that was. Could it be a job? She sat down and finished her coffee and then decided to mop the dusty floor and Windex the glass doors before getting ready for the mystery appointment.

Seated in the chair on the non-working side of the desk in Kendra's office, after a formal greeting, Shelly decided it couldn't be about a job. Kendra looked too serious. Shelly wondered why she had bothered to take the extra time to try to look professional. Kendra looked at her as if she should know what the meeting was about. Shelly raised her eyebrows in inquiry.

"It's about Carmel," Kendra said.

Shelly felt the blood draining away from her face. She hadn't heard her daughter's name in over five years. Since Frank left. Was this the moment she had always feared? That what you fear the most will meet you half way. She didn't know where that line came from, but it popped into her head from somewhere. She swayed in her chair.

Kendra jumped up and said, "Put your head down between your knees. Don't faint away on me, Shelly." She pushed Shelly's back down firmly so that her head hung down. Kendra patted Shelly's shoulder and said, "Hold on."

Shelly held on. One hand gripped each knee as though relying on them for support. She let her head hang and attempted to draw breath. She managed small staccato gasps. She flashed back to dropping her head earlier in the day at her kitchen table. She was much lower now and didn't think she had it in her to rise again. It would be easier not to fight gravity and just continue down onto the floor. She leaned forward and yearned to let her face rest on the cool tiles.

Kendra stopped this movement by grabbing Shelly's shoulders. "Okay, Shelly let's get you up again," she said firmly.

Shelly didn't have the strength to resist. She sat up again and leaned back hard against the chair and closed her eyes. She swallowed loudly, squeezed her eyes tighter shut and managed to stammer, "Is sh-she. . ."

"Oh, Shelly, I'm so sorry," Kendra said.

Shelly felt her body lose its definition. She started to dissolve into liquid remorse.

Kendra continued, "I'm sorry to have frightened you. Carmel is. . .well, as all right as she can be under the circumstances."

Shelly opened her eyes and began to reinhabit her body. She looked at Kendra and said, "She's n-not. . ."

"She's definitely alive, though she's still, uh. . ." Kendra let the sentence stop.

Shelly finished it. "Using," she said.

Kendra nodded.

"That is as I expected," Shelly said. "We tried every possibility we could come up with to wean her off her high, but we didn't manage to help her."

Kendra nodded. "When was the last time you saw her," she asked.

"It's been over five years," Shelly said. "We exhausted every resource we could dig up and then some. Her father and I didn't know how to live with each other after we finally came to the conclusion that we were unable to help her. I don't think we blamed each other, as much as we saw constant reminders of our failure as parents and guardians when we were together. I haven't seen or heard from Carmel or Frank in all this time."

Kendra nodded.

Shelly closed her eyes and sighed. She had never told anyone else about this. These few terse sentences seemed to open up room in her chest for her to breathe.

She savoured this relief for a moment and then frowned. She asked, "So, what about Carmel, then? She's using and I'm sorry and sad, but I've come to realize I can't change that. I've had to let her go." The last thought always made her want to wail out loud. Keening, they used to call it. Like mourners at wakes in the olden days, who would rend their clothes, rub ashes into their skin and howl like wounded animals, like banshees, whatever those were.

"Carmel has a son," Kendra said.

Shelly stilled. She swallowed in an attempt to bring moisture to her suddenly dry mouth. With a wince, she asked, "Is he...uh, okay?"

"He seems to be."

Shelly felt blood pour into her face when she realized she was a grandmother. It wasn't anything she had even considered before. She felt altered, somehow. "What is. . .how old. . .who is. . ." she stammered.

Kendra said, "His name is Jackson. He is almost a year old."

Shelly nodded while conflicting thoughts ricocheted round her head. A quick picture of a cigarette package flickered in her mind. She remembered her daughter smoked Peter Jackson brand and guessed that was where she came up with the baby's name. Was his father named Peter? Would anyone ever know? And then one big question crowded out the others. Looking at Kendra, Shelly asked, "How can Carmel be a mother?"

"That's where we come in, Shelly. Carmel can't be a mother. Sure, she gave birth, but she's not even close to being a competent caregiver."

Shelly still wondered if she had been a competent caregiver to her errant daughter. Her mind was short-circuiting with conflicting thoughts and emotions.

"Jackson is in our care. Social Services," Kendra said.

Shelly's eyes widened and her heart hurt. Burned. She placed her right hand over the fire in her chest and asked, "How long?"

"Just this week," Kendra answered.

Shelly tilted her head to one side. She was trying to reason out her grandson's fraught existence.

"Carmel had a roommate. She was Jackson's primary caregiver and probably Carmel's too. A good-hearted woman who looked after them both, but she is in hospice care now and she realized that she had to let us know about Jackson's situation."

Shelly realized that her face was wet. She hadn't felt them falling, but it must be tears. Her grandson's precarious home life hit a nerve. The dying woman who had looked after her daughter and grandson touched her. She would not sob. She would not. Unfelt tears didn't count. She had promised herself years ago to shed no more tears for her lost daughter. She took short, small breaths, which were definitely not sobs.

"So, can you take him?" Kendra asked.

Shelly's breath stopped altogether. Her mind hadn't progressed through all of the obvious implications. Finally, she gasped, and gulped. "I...uh, I..."

"He's your grandson. We don't know his father, so there are no other relatives. If not you, we will approach Frank and his new wife."

Shelly jumped up. "I need a break. Give me a minute or two," she said and walked out of the office without waiting for a reply. Looking around, but not taking anything in, she paced the empty hallway and wished she still smoked. When a washroom sign registered in her mind, she went in and splashed cool water on her face. Leaning hard on the vanity while studying her reflection for answers, she attempted to take calming breaths.

When she returned from the restroom, Shelly said to Kendra, "Can I have a day to think it through? It is a lot to take in."

Kendra nodded. "Twenty-four hours and if I haven't heard from you, I will contact Frank. I'm guessing he and his new wife won't want to be bothered with a baby and that leaves...Foster Care."

Shelly gulped aloud. "Is he here?"

"No, but I can take you to see him now."

Shelly nodded. She guessed her stunned expression mirrored the one she had worn when she discovered her working days were coming to an end.

Kendra suggested they both go in her car, which worked because Shelly wasn't sure her mind could cope with driving when it was consumed with so much else. She had no idea where they were or how they had gotten there, when Kendra parked and led her into a townhouse much like her own.

On autopilot she stumbled behind Kendra into a kitchen that had sunlight shining through sliding glass doors. Shaking her head to clear this surreal development, she reached down and felt her skirt to reassure herself that she wasn't still at home in her bathrobe. This kitchen must face west, unlike hers which faced east. Her eyes registered the smudges on the glass and then moved over to focus on the small smudge-maker who stood with one small hand pressed up against the door. A pool of drool caught the light below his bottom lip.

Shelly sighed.

A Good Listener

By Laura MacCourt

Laced with warm sunshine, the cone-tipped pine boughs lifted and waved. Where the golden light reached the ground, fresh white trilliums offered their dewy petals of three. Their crowded masses transformed the ground into a carpet of white, alive and strong. Finches and chickadees, robins and redwings added to the pines' wind song with their own rhythmic, territorial songs. A drowsy bee searched and darted about, while chipmunks rustled in the leaves, taking little care for silence, and searching for remembered caches of acorns.

The dried winter grasses lay flattened on the earth, stem upon stem, matted with endless leaves whose autumn journey spiraled downward, each in its many-coloured coat, to rest forever. Here and there around them, new seedlings peered cautiously, then, encouraged by the sun, bravely reached higher. Ground covers, aspiring to no particular height, began to wander and explore beyond last season's boundaries. Everything, *everything*, was awake and growing or preparing to be born, searching for its place or meaning in the spring woods.

An old rail fence, lichen-covered and vine-wrapped, also wandered through the woods, in a path generally straight, though curiously bent at times. Perhaps its builder, enjoying a fine bit of gossip or hearty laugh, unwittingly allowed its path to stray. Eventually this fence crossed a small meadow where even more sunlight touched the trilliums. The shady side of the fence, still sheltered by pines and oaks, was cool and softly lit with violets.

It was here, at this fence, that I first met the young lad. I'd listened to and watched him for some time, coming ever closer, thwacking dry twigs from their solid trunks, ringing old and clinging oak leaves like wind chimes, and knighting virtually anything whether it moved or not. The stick, half as tall as he, looked like any other, but in his hand, the power and imagination he knew seemed to emanate from it.

He was small and freckled, dressed in new overalls, and shoes that had once been white, with no socks beneath them. A cap was pulled snugly over his thick red hair. He travelled wide-eyed and full of energy, for every moment offered the possibility of a new adventure.

Before he saw me, he turned suddenly and flung the stick high and far away, then stooped to snatch up some dry wild grasses that waved all around his feet. I was wondering when he might finally notice me, if at all. He did, and came running with great pleasure toward the fence. With little effort, he leaped up on the top rail, straddled it a moment, then curled in his legs and feet for balance. We looked at one another with instant friendship. I've always been a good listener. People will impart wonderful ideas and feelings and truths, *if* you don't interrupt them, and I sensed this lad was brimming with unspoken words that he was eager to share with me.

"I'm Teddy, and we just moved here. We live in the brown house across from the great big wheat field. I never lived in the country before. It sure is big and wild — so was the city, but not like this! I can explore for hours, and no one minds. There's fish in the creek, and deer come out from the edge of the woods at dark. I watch them from my bedroom window.

"And quiet! The loudest sound out here is the wind. Oh, yeah, and the rooster next door, *and* all the donkeys down the road!

"Do you ever look at all the stars? I try counting them, but there aren't enough numbers for that. Maybe I'll invent more when I'm older. A lot of people may want to know how many stars there are. I do. You know what else I want to do? Climb trees. We've got a couple of apple trees, but right now they're all covered with blossoms. When those apples are ripe, I'll be up there filling my pockets. Maybe we can eat some together. I'm glad you live here, too. Bet I'm the first boy to come by all morning. When I make some friends, we'll all come here, and maybe follow this fence to see how far it goes. Just until dinner, though. My mom's the best cook, and dad's going to hunt wild turkeys. Everybody's happier here than in the city. Even my baby sister, I guess, except she cries a lot, unless she's asleep. Marie's only a few weeks old, so it'll be awhile before she can come out with me. That's why I've got to make some friends. You'll be my first one."

I looked at my new friend, who paused at last for a breath and to reposition his hat which had on its brim the words, "Just Ask Me." This was not necessary. Everything about him made me want to follow him away from this place, wherever he went, to climb a tree if I could, or to help him get farther up one if he climbed on me first, and *certainly* to eat all of those promised apples. I loved him, and hoped with all my heart that he *would* come, often, and bring every detail of every moment of his day. As I told you, I'm a good listener, not much for conversation. There is more to be learned from listening than from wagging one's tongue.

Still, I wish I could have found the words to tell him how different my life was from his. My home was one of fear and nervousness, of endurance and toil, of beatings and long fasts without food and water. Of *never* giving up hope of being rescued. Of suffering in silence.

The joy of being young and free and cared for had blinded Teddy to my misfortunes. Away from the violence afflicting me, I was as free as my spirit, at least, could wander. Restored was I, minute by minute, as he chattered away, requiring no reply from me. I understood what I could, and was patient with the rest. Some days my head hung low, and my legs barely held me up, but they carried me to that fence in time for a daily rendezvous with the one bright hope that remained in my very different world. At times, I wanted to lie down in the soft new undergrowth, but feared I might not will myself to rise up. Only if the lad stopped coming, only then would I give in to that rest. From deep within my heart, I knew and believed that this life of mine was not as it should be. Faint memories reminded me that things had not always been this harsh. Would anyone ever intervene on my behalf? Would they be in time?

Somehow, miraculously, Teddy *did* come to understand. Eager to share our friendship with his father, Teddy brought him to see me one morning. I liked that man instantly. He was very much like his son, and his voice and touch were incredibly gentle. I had forgotten such gestures, and believed they existed only in dreams. Most important of all, his eyes saw instantly what Teddy's had not.

One day, soon after, I was taken on a visit to their home for the first time. All three of us walked along the road, with me in the middle, but slowly because I was still very sore. I was just able to keep up with them. And what a feast of food and drink, laughter and kind people were waiting for me! May this moment last forever, I wished.

And this wish came true. They wanted me to stay! I certainly gave no argument. Their home became mine, their happiness, too. Teddy and I explored as far as we dared all the beautiful, welcoming countryside. I had been very young and, I think, even loved, when last I had freedom to traverse those country roads with my fellow creatures. Our only boundary was that old rail fence. Beyond it was my old life, never to be revisited. My wounds and spirit healed quickly. Thanks to my new friend, I felt like the frisky colt I had once been. By day, I might gallop with pleasure instead of in fear and, by night, doze placidly in my warm, freshly strawed stall.

Teddy and his family restored my faith in humanity. That lad still has plenty of ideas to share with me each morning, and enough to last until we say good night. I suppose thoughts even occur to him in his sleep. This is not so with me. My sleep is uninterrupted and peaceful, and my days content and carefree. The mouth-watering crunch of oats and hay between my teeth, the long drinks of cool, clear water, and the many cheerful swallows that live in the barn with me are just a few of the simple pleasures in this thoroughly happy new life of mine.

I am quite certain that Teddy saved my life. Being a good listener has its rewards, you know. Apples, for starters.

Love at:

By Lori Pearson

Love at 25

Let me love you again
The time will never be right
Within the confines of months or years or today
Let me love you again
Meaning forever confined to today
The birth of our emotion
May be imminent
I want to touch you
To teach you who you are
In much the same way
That I want to be touched
And taught just what it is I am
Neither truly succeeds
We are so young.
Let me love you again
Time need not be a factor
We love, therefore become eternal
For love will never die

Love at 45

Let me love you again
I have sought throughout the years
Someone who in quality of spirit
Meets me equally
A climax in the soul
But when I promised forever
I didn't know I meant forever, confined to today
And when you touched me
I was filled with light
But when I touched you
I left jagged scars
We are not so young
That we can afford the luxury of time
The eternity of loss
Eclipses the illusion of love
And only the barest of threads
Says love will never die.

Love at 55

I have loved you always
I just didn't know I could.
And I will love you always
Like I always thought I would

Elegy

By Lori Pearson

I yearn too much for the physical
To hold a lock of your hair and smell its fragrance
To place my hand over yours lining them up together
My nose buried into the soft part behind your ear
The warmth of your early morning embrace

I keep your leather gloves
That mimic your hands, search photographs curiously for the
veins and sinews I recall
I put a dab of your aftershave on my wrist
Burrow deep in the blankets, contorted not with lust but sobs
I yearn too much for the physical

I yearn too much for the spiritual
Wondering if you are a twinkle in the sky like a star
Which is some big rock in space and not an interesting place
to be at all
So I think about you at the beach, in the wind, in my heart
Laughter, rain, thunder, flavour, delight
You are so special you elude me in the perfection
of places you could be
Anywhere but gone, I cry

I look for you in familiar things and places
Listen to your voice on tape, messages in music
The play of light, you in the corner of my eye
Disappearing before I fully recognize you
Our private jokes, I laugh alone,
you chuckle softly in my soul
And for a second, I feel whole
Anywhere but gone, I cry
I yearn too much for the spiritual

I yearn too much for you
The safe harbour that was your embrace
A neophyte you called me and educated me in all your ways
And I was as much you as I could be
I loved as much as was ever able
At peace, we slid apart, that line crossed
Between life and death
Your love for me, in your very last breath

And my love for you, that peeling potatoes kind of plight
To take a step forward through this endless night
I am still as much you as I am able
I hold you like a light to see my way
And the only thing I am able to believe
Is there is no end, we will be together again
For without that solidly in my gut
I could not take another step
I yearn too much for you.

Finding Arthur (excerpt)
Visit to the Aunties in Aberdeen, 1981

By Carole Payne

I awoke in the morning surprised, not only that I hadn't been cold all night, but that I had actually slept deeply. I yawned and stretched and opened my eyes to see Eadie's frame in the doorway, telling me to wake up because my breakfast was on the table. The bed may have been warm but when I put my feet on the floor it was freezing and I could see my breath as I hurried into my clothes and into the warmth of the kitchen. A hot pot of tea and soft-boiled eggs and toast with a slice of tomato were set out for me. I glanced at the clock. Nine already.

"Are you not eating, Auntie?"

"I've eaten already. I let you sleep in this morning but I expect you to get up earlier when you are here for the rest of the week."

She was signalling who was in charge of this visit. Once again I made a note that she would be the one who decided what she would tell me and when. And what she would keep me from knowing. As if reading my thoughts, she produced my itinerary for the next four days.

"I have to go into the shop this morning. One of my better customers has a wedding she needs a fancy frock for. You'll come with me and I will show you the shop before she comes. Then you can go to Esslemont and Macintosh's on the High Street and visit some of the other stores. You can pick up some chops for dinner and walk home from there. I will give you the directions. It is not far.

"On Friday night, Louis has said he will take you to the synagogue. I don't go anymore. I can't climb the stairs, but I gave them a substantial amount for the new building when they had to move from the old. It is very pretty. Lena will go with you and sit with you in the women's section. They don't have a rabbi now. The congregation is too small." She looked at me and added, almost under her breath, "I hope you have brought something appropriate to wear."

Seeing that I was about to ask more about the synagogue, she intercepted with, "We don't have time for questions now. Eat up your breakfast. We have to get going very soon. Louis will tell you all about the shul. You can think about things you want to see in Aberdeen before you go."

I cleared the dishes and put them in the sink. I donned all the winter clothes I had brought to Aberdeen this cold January and after a short ride we were at her store, Edith Lann, Modiste, a fancy dress shop that I had memories of from the last time I had been here when I was eleven. Then I had been taken along as my mother was fitted out with fine dresses until she had finally settled on one or two. The store was the same in 1981 as it had been in 1953 and probably as it had been when Eadie had bought it in the 1930s. Much to my chagrin, this time I, who hated shopping for anything, especially clothes, was made to submit to trying on fancy frocks from Paris and London.

"I don't do it so much any more, but I used to make regular trips to buy the best from Europe. That's how I built up my clientele over the years. They knew if they came to me they would have the highest quality and most up to date fashions. They have been very loyal."

One look at the prices convinced me of why my aunt was still in business and why I would be broke if I bought anything here. It didn't take very long for Eadie to realize that neither she nor I would be happy with my wearing anything in the store. I think she was genuinely disappointed that I didn't share my mother's flair for clothes but she was quick enough to see that she wasn't going to get a sale and let me go with instructions to be home in time for supper and where to get the chops.

When we sat down to eat, I noted that the refrigerator was back in the kitchen. She looked surprised at my observation.

"Don't you remember when we came when I was eleven and Uncle Eddie was here from New York and he couldn't |believe that granny didn't have a fridge and that she had to buy things fresh every day and keep them cool in the scullery? I remember that day so well, the day that the new refrigerator was delivered and was brought into the kitchen and Uncle Eddie had already decided where it would go and how the men put it right there against that wall under the clock, away from the heater, and they plugged it in and everyone except granny was excited because now the house was going to be modern. After it was running for a while, Uncle Eddie brought out all the perishable things from the scullery and put them in the fridge. He was very pleased with himself. I remember that. He said that he wanted granny's life to be easier and that is why he had done it. Do you remember?"

"I don't remember all of that but I do remember your granny's reaction."

"Me too. As soon as he had left to go back to America, she unplugged it.

"And she never used it again. But when she died. . ." She paused. Granny had died in 1954, but the look on Eadie's face had the immediacy of grief writ large. If they had seen my grandfather as a mixed blessing, all of her children, as far as I could discern, had loved my granny without reservation. Eadie came back to the moment, "When she died, I plugged it in again and I've used it since. I haven't thought about that story for a long time. It doesn't cost very much to run and it does save shopping every day. Eddie was right all those years ago."

After dinner, at my request, we went round the house,

looking at everything. It was not so grand as I remembered. My biggest disappointment was the scullery, or pantry. What I remembered as a cupboard of delights seemed just ordinary now. The garden, although small, had been my granny's pride. I remembered the flowers and the mint.

"There has not been much of anything there for a long time," Eadie said.

It didn't feel like there was much life in the house, either. More like old people and ghosts of people and times past. The few pictures were still on the walls. The house was solid enough, but I guessed that Eadie's life was in the store and with her sister Lena and with Louis.

We continued to sit in the kitchen after supper was cleared up. She wanted to know about my life in Canada and about the children and my husband, Don. After she was satisfied with that, she wanted to know about my mom. "You said she was still very unhappy when she died."

This could be difficult, I thought. "Yes. She had been drinking again and she was on her own and she just couldn't cope. Gordon gave up her apartment in the end and she was in a nursing home and then in the hospital when she was really sick. Then she died." I couldn't bring myself to tell Eadie that I had broken off all relationship with my mom before the end.

"A nursing home?" Eadie appeared shocked. "She would have only been in her sixties. How could Gordon have put her with old sick people?"

I was beginning to squirm. I wanted to say that my mom had not been nice. I wanted to tell her sister that in fact she had been impossible. I wanted to tell her about the overdoses and the visits to the hospital to have her stomach pumped out and the endless calls to me when she had still been in the apartment and the lack of support from Don and the toll on our family of her constant demands, of my emotional exhaustion, the damage to our kids because of the stress upon me. But I said nothing.

How could I tell this stranger, sister to my mother, that in the last few months I had had a change of heart about my understanding of who this person, Minnie, my mother, actually had been before she died? How could I explain how my hatred towards her and my love for Gordon, the man who I had always thought was my father, had been so profoundly affected by the revelations of the last few months? Secrets had kept us all apart from each other, had opened a wide gulf between families that might now be bridged — but there was no guarantee of this either. It had been so long in the making, this gulf between us. We were suspended over the abyss of silence. I was increasingly aware that she was afraid of telling me what I needed to know and that I might not find out if we did not tread carefully. I did not know what had happened between my parents so I couldn't comment on my aunt's accusations. I waited.

"I stayed in contact with her all those years. She didn't complain about her life. But she never seemed to have financial independence. I would send her money from time to time. Her writing did deteriorate at the end so I knew she was no longer herself. It is so sad."

I was stunned with these sudden revelations. I had no idea that there had been any communication between the families since we had been summarily sent home when the extent of my mother's drinking had been discovered when I was eleven. And money being sent to my mom...was Gordon not looking after her? Was she being manipulative so she could have extra money for booze? What did the Scottish relatives know about what was really going on in Canada? What did they know about me? I did not say anything.

Eadie moved to safer ground. "Your mother was so full of life when she was young. She was energetic and pretty, and swept Arthur off his feet! Now that was a wedding to go to! I remember it well. Such a party! Your granny never drank —

but on that night she drank so much with happiness for them. It was the only time I ever saw her drunk!"

She got up and rummaged in a drawer. After a moment, she pulled out a small framed sepia photograph of a man and a woman, she sitting on his knee, he with his arm around her shoulder, eyes of both sparkling. "That's Minnie and Arthur on the day of their engagement." I catch my breath. I have never seen this picture. My mother's hair is dark not blonde. It is only the third image I have seen of my father. Eadie takes the picture back, looks at it again, struggles for an instant and says, "I am an old woman and that has been sitting in this house since 1936. I don't need it any more. You can have it if you like."

As she hands it back to me, I am overwhelmed once again, with emotions that are too big for me to comprehend. They fill every part of me and overflow into tears that won't stop. Eadie is clearly not used to displays of such raw emotion. She keeps moving without acknowledging the tears.

"Your father was such a lovely man, so kind and gentle. He loved Minnie and worshipped and adored her. He would have done anything for her — and he did. Did you know that he converted to marry your mother? Do you know what that means for an Orthodox Jewish male?"

I nodded miserably. "Yes, Uncle Benny told me about the circumcision."

She snorted. "Imagine a twenty-six-year-old grown man losing all his common sense for love and undergoing circumcision at that age? He was totally crazy!" She stopped and filled up her teacup. "But he did love her."

Netless

By Ann Partridge

"That makes ten, Ethan," Seth said as he pulled their string out of the stream and fastened a slippery trout to it. Crouching on the bank, he wiped his slimy hands on the grass. "Eight speckles and two browns. That should feed everybody."

Leaning back against a tree trunk, Ethan stretched his arms over his head. He yawned and then said, "Let's go for a dozen, man. If we head back now we'll have to do the milking and mucking out."

"But if we're not back for chores, Cassie and Emma'll have to do 'em. Then my old man will go on a rant and send the girls fishing next time. This here's the only job that don't feel like work," Seth said. He stood holding the string of fish and looking impatient.

Ethan yawned again. "Yeah, I know, but I'm beat. Thomas made it home and we were up half the night."

"Wh-what?" Seth asked with wide eyes. He lowered the fish back into the cool running water, secured the string and sat down on the bank facing his friend. "Why didn't you say before?"

"I've been thinking about some of the things he told us and ... well, it's kinda scary. He's my big brother and I don't think he would lie to me, but I'm having trouble believing his stories about how things are out there." Ethan waved around them to indicate the broader world.

"Like what?" Seth asked. He watched Ethan intensely, seeking any telltale clues of fabrication. His friend wasn't above making up a big story to get out of doing chores.

Closing his eyes, Ethan said, "Well first of all Thomas

looks like a famine victim."

"What? But he's a big strong guy, a football player and everything...Why? How?" Seth sputtered his surprise.

"Part of it is because he walked home."

"All the way from college? Why would he do that? He usually rides the Greyhound. Is he out of money? Wouldn't one of his friends give him a lift at least part way?"

"There are no buses or trains running and no one has money, not even the banks, apparently. So, Thomas says, anyhow. He had a bicycle for a bit, but a bigger guy knocked him off it and took it."

"B-but..." A stunned Seth wrinkled his forehead and shook his head before speaking again. "But that can't be right. Okay, we know the Net went down a few months, must be five months ago now, and we haven't been back to school... Never thought I'd miss it, but it was better than working every day. I said something to my old man about child labour laws and he said thirteen years old ain't no child. Anyway on the radio they say that they will have everything organized again soon, so..."

Ethan nodded. He had had the same information until last night. "Thomas says that is government prop-propo-something to keep people from panicking. It's a lie."

Seth's mouth moved, but no words came forth.

Ethan watched his friend try to take all this in. Taking a deep breath, he continued, "It wasn't just the Net that went out, it was other electronic communications, too – satellites and stuff. Thomas says that the banks have lost track of the money 'cause most of it was just numbers on a computer, not greenbacks. They can't be sure if someone messed with their records before everything crashed. So with the banks closed, almost no one has money, now."

Seth gripped his hands together hard and hunched his shoulders as if warding off blows.

"And even if someone had a pile of cash buried in their

back yard, there isn't anything to buy with it. There is no food nowhere in the cities 'less somebody had a stocked pantry, Thomas said. He ate 'til he upchucked last night. Ma said he's only to take a little at a time 'cause his stomach ain't used to it."

Seth rocked forwards and back for a few moments in silence. Stopping suddenly, he looked hard at Ethan and asked, "Is this another one of your tall tales to keep me from headin' home? It is, isn't it?"

Ethan shook his head wearily. "I wish it was. You can come over and peek in at Thomas when we get back. He's likely still sleeping. Ma says he got to stay in bed and rest or he'll come down real sick. He stayed up there at that school with his friends 'cause they thought it would just be maybe a week until everything was back to normal. But now, he says, there is no normal. He says crowds of people are heading out of the cities and looking for places to find food and Daddy says we will need to be on guard 'cause desperate people will do pretty near anything to survive. Thomas said crowds smashed into grocery stores and just took everything they could carry and all the stores are empty now. He said there's no gas at gas stations 'cause they can't get ahold of the companies or the trucks or something."

Seth started rocking again. "I feel funny, like everything's tilted."

Ethan nodded in agreement.

"I never knew that every damn thing depended on the damn internet," Seth said with feeling.

"Yeah. We only used it at school, so not much changed for us. The folks must have had an idea, though, because I've never seen them so serious about growing vegetables and not wasting anything and working every hour every day. Now Daddy says we're lucky 'cause we grow most of our food and we've got chickens, pigs, cows and milk and such. I thought it was just a lot of work, but it would be worse wandering around all day and not havin' any grub."

Frowning in concentration, Seth was silent for a while. "Maybe I ain't flunkin' English anymore," he said with a wry grin.

Ethan tried a smile, too, glad to let some of the seriousness slip away. He opened his mouth to offer another good point, but looking beyond Seth he let out an "Ooof!" sound.

Turning around to see what his friend saw, Seth jumped to his feet and with cartwheeling arms just stopped himself from toppling down the bank and into the creek.

An unfamiliar woman was standing in the stream with her arms outstretched and face and open palms pointing in their direction. She had blond hair parted in the middle and seemed to be naked, though she was submerged to just below the shoulders. She didn't say anything, just stared. The current didn't seem to affect her, she stood absolutely still.

Where did she come from, Seth wondered as he cleared his throat nervously. "Uh, m-ma'am, do you need, uh, help?" He moved to step into the water to go to her aid.

"Stop, Seth!" Ethan called.

Seth turned to look at his friend. Ethan was standing with his net in one hand, and the other in a fist. That was the quickest he had moved all day, Seth thought. "What?" he said, while pointing with his eyes toward the woman in the water.

"Look how skinny her arms are. She's hungry. Remember what I said about desperate people?" Ethan said harshly.

Seth looked at the immobile woman and then back at his friend.

In the same voice, Ethan instructed, "Look at her unfocused stare."

Seth looked. It was an oddly vacant gaze. "Maybe she's blind or she lost her glasses and can't see," he suggested and turned back to Ethan.

"That's exactly right," Ethan said. "But not the way you mean. Thomas told me about them. He said lots of people wore something called Google glasses which connected them to the internet as long as their eyes were open all day long. That stare means she was among the most addicted Netheads. He said he even knew some people who had them for a long time and they ended up living online more and more than in the real world and they eventually lost all their uh, like human feelings and eventually they felt no connection to the rest of the world. They lived entirely in cyberspace and would go off and just sit in a corner and hope someone would feed them and remind them to take a shower and brush their teeth and other ordinary stuff." Dropping his voice to a whisper he said, "They sometimes even crapped themselves."

Seth grimaced. "But it's been months. Maybe she's better now and she just needs a little help."

"Does she look better to you?"

Seth looked at the unmoving woman with the unnerving stare. He shook his head. "She looks like a st-statue. Maybe, she's frozen."

"Water's not that cold."

"Well, we can't just leave her there."

"We can, Seth. We will. Think about it. How did she get here?" Ethan asked.

Seth looked up and down and across the stream and then lifted both shoulders.

"Well she can get somewhere else the same way she showed up to scare the fish away."

"B-but..."

"Maybe when we're gone, she'll think the video has ended and she'll find another spot where something is moving."

Seth looked from the still staring woman to Ethan and back again.

"B-but, I, uh, I wanted to help her and...I, uh, n-never

saw a b-barenaked. . ." Seth looked down at his feet when he felt heat in his face.

"You have. Mind when we had that supply teacher than left us on our own for over an hour with the internet on."

Seth nodded and continued to blush. "But not in real life."

"She'd think it was realer than life."

They both turned to look at the woman in the water.

They saw ripples radiating out from around her as she slowly rose up out of the water. As the boys had anticipated she was naked, at least from the waist up. After that, however, was a frightening revelation. Below the waist she appeared to be heavily muscled ... and green. It was definitely not a fish tail like say, a mermaid, because she also sported a large olive-hued erection.

Ethan backed into the tree. Hard. He dropped his net. Seth let out a gasp that was nearly a shriek and ran towards the path for home. Ethan caught and passed him before he had gotten far.

When she was sure they were gone, Lysandra removed the bottom of the grotesque, but anatomically correct, Hulk costume from around her waist. When she had shoved it in her backpack at the abandoned adult costume store, she had just wanted some weight in her bag. Carrying the green rubber monstrosity in one hand, she walked over and retrieved the poles, net and the string of fish forgotten by the boys and then turned back in the direction of her hidden camp. Nethead maybe, but she was learning survival skills.

Autumn

By Lori Pearson

Autumn crept in prematurely.
My soul, not yet ready to relinquish
the warmth of summer or the promise of spring.
Unyielding, I erected barriers within myself
as formidable as the thunderclouds and cold winds
that coloured and swept the leaves away.
And as my eyes swept the barren beach
that one last time, a small child running toward the waves,
joyously chased away the fears of
a heart leaning toward winter.
A seagull feather caressed by crippled hands
with the softness of sand and clouds and sun.
Victory in each rollicking wave, tickling a shore
filled with summer laughter.
The immortality of the seasons became
mine in that moment of
a child at play, impervious to the gloom and chill
of an autumn night.
I live forever on the shore of the lake
in the seagull's cry, in the last shaft of light on a summer's day.

From Bernardo Boy to Man of Leisure

By Ellen Curry

True story of Terrance George Harrison as told to Ellen Curry.

Britain was having a terrible time after the end of World War II. Many families – thousands among them led by single mothers whose husbands never made it back from the war – were finding it hard just to feed their children.

Terrance George's mother, then only in her early twenties, was living with her four children in a shed at the bottom of her sister's garden, a piece of land fifteen feet by twelve, barely large enough to grow vegetables for one family, let alone two. But Mrs. George had heard about a man named Barnardo, a doctor and philanthropist who'd founded an organisation that sent children from destitute families to live and work in Australia or Canada. Both were young countries with small populations and were glad to take in the children, who were placed on farms where they were given board and lodging in exchange for their labour.

Mrs. George's heart was heavy when she gave up Terrance to what is now known as Dr. Barnardo's Homes. She knew she would never see him again, but at least he wouldn't starve or have to fend for a living on the streets of London. He would be placed on a ship bound for Canada.

Terrance was only five when he left his homeland and doesn't remember much about his mother, except the sight of her standing at the train station with tears in her eyes and his younger brother and twin sister clinging to her skirts.

He'd never been on a train before, only seen them hurtling by on the tracks at the end of the road, and the ride was exciting as the English countryside flew past the windows. The children, lost in their own thoughts as night came, fell asleep sitting up. When morning arrived, they were taken off the train and marched the short distance to the ship.

On board, they were restricted to one area, crowded with other boys and a few girls all about Terrance's age. Terrance was, understandably, homesick. And he was afraid of the water – he had never seen much of it before – and spent most of the Atlantic crossing being seasick. So he was more than pleased when they saw land, with trees, trees and more trees, all green, so much better than being surrounded by that blue terrifying water.

Terrance was placed on the Harrison farm in Roseneath, with a close-knit family – father, mother and three girls, two older than Terrance and one a year younger. He was a good boy, big for his age and eager to learn and he made sure that whatever task he was given was done well. He came to be the son that they never had. They called him Terry.

Mrs. Harrison was home-schooling the girls and at night, when the work was done, Mavis and Sally loved to play school with Terry as their pupil. Soon he was reading as well as his teachers and it was a proud moment for him when he could take his turn at the family's Sunday Bible readings. They all loved his English accent.

As he'd arrived with only one set of clothes, his new mother made him new ones out of Mr. Harrison's cast-offs. Terry had never been so well off – now he had three sets of clothes: two for work and one for Sundays.

Once every two weeks, Terry would help load the donkey with baskets containing the extra vegetables they had and could exchange with the neighbour for pork and bacon or whatever the other farmer had extra. Terry enjoyed this time walking beside the donkey with father Harrison; with just the two of them it was quality time, he could ask questions and they would not be interrupted. Not that he didn't love the girls as sisters, but there were times that they acted just plain silly.

At the end of every month Terry would leave the farm before dawn and carry a bag of corn all the way to the mill in Cobourg. It was a long and tedious day for a young boy. The bag was heavy, weighing nearly as much as he did. But his family depended on him and he was determined to do his share. While waiting for the corn to be milled into flour to be carried back home, he would go rabbit hunting on the land that's now home to Cobourg Creek Golf Course. He'd always return home to the farm with several rabbits he'd shot, and sometimes that was the only meat the family had.

The Mill played an extremely important part in the growth of Cobourg, without it many of the farmers and their families would have starved. The farms were small, some just a few acres. It was a hard tough life and the farmers needed the extra hands to scrape out a living for their families.

The Harrisons could not have loved Terry more had he been their own son and he in turn loved the family as if it was his own. The girls married and left home but Terry stayed on with the couple, and when there was not enough farm work, he went to work at the local hardware store, where he met Susan and fell in love. They married and had a home of their own, but he still took time to take care of the old couple until their death.

By the time Terry could afford a trip back to England, his brothers and sisters had passed away and he didn't see much point in making the journey.

As a poor young farm boy making those trips to the mill, he'd never dreamed of himself being retired and playing golf or marshalling on the course where he'd shot so many rabbits. He now was a man of leisure.

Terry has passed on now, but he had a good life, happily married for forty-eight years with three children and six grandchildren. How different his life would have been had he stayed in England. Although it must have been heart-wrenching for his mother to give him away, she knew that he stood the chance of a much better life in Canada.

A Learning Experience

By Mary Soni

I'm going to tell you a story. Maybe you'll learn something. Maybe it will just entertain you for a while as you read it, and then you'll go on with your life and forget all about it. I hope you learn from it, but either way, I mostly hope you enjoy it...

There was a girl who loved a boy. Not necessarily the dating, groping, hooking up kind of love: she would have been content just being friends. She was a special girl, she was fiercely loyal to her few friends and she loved them all, in her way. But her specialness made her different, and so people didn't always pay much attention to her or in fact notice her at all. She noticed everything, however, and remembered most of what she noticed. Sometimes it helped her when she could remember all those things, but most often everything rattling around in her head was very distracting, and it made it hard to focus on things that weren't taking place inside her own head. She had a very vivid imagination as well, and was always making up stories. Most of these never got written down anywhere; she just told them to herself silently, jumping from one to the next whenever her fancy took her, sometimes returning to an old one, other times coming up with something completely new. Because of all this she was somewhat withdrawn, and didn't talk to others much.

At school her grades were good enough, because even though she had trouble relating to others and getting her thoughts across, she retained everything she read and heard, so she did all right on tests and assignments.

At her job placement she did well enough, when she could focus on the outside world long enough, without retreating back inside herself (she mostly did this in times of stress).

At home she lived rather simply, to her. Her room was cluttered and messy, and she would never get rid of anything or give anything away (she even refused to lend pencils and pens at school), but it was how she liked it. She spent most of her time reading, or playing video games, which she immensely enjoyed but it never occurred to her that these solitary activities only increased her isolation. Of course if she had realized she probably wouldn't have cared anyway.

Now this boy was not like her. He had lots of friends, and girlfriends. He did very well at school and had no troubles at work. He was funny, and smart, and good-looking. And, like most people their age, he could have a good time when he wanted to.

The girl knew that others sometimes went to parties, and smoked, and drank, and did other things. She heard them all talk at school, about where they had been, and who had done what. But none of that interested her at all. So she just listened, and while she absorbed, and remembered, she didn't really pay much more attention to it than that. She also knew that the boy did go to parties and things as well, but she didn't care. She still loved him.

She didn't even realize at first that she did, in fact, love him. She knew she noticed him a lot more than she noticed anything or anyone else, and she knew that she found him just as funny and smart and nice as anyone else did. She knew that she knew more about him than she did about most other people she knew, just from listening to him talk to his friends. But it never occurred to her that all of this might be part of loving him. Until one day when she was reading yet another book, and in that book they were talking about love. She read that, and thought about it, and then she decided that she loved this boy. Not necessarily the same kind of love that you or I would feel for someone, but, in her way, she loved him. Of course she also immediately knew she would never do or say anything about it, but that was just her way.

One day, however, something happened. Something that changed her completely, and shook up her way of viewing the world.

She had heard that there was going to be another party. She ignored all the chatter, of course, because it did not matter to her. She had heard also that he was going to the party, which she did pay attention to. She heard that it was a beach party, and some of them were bringing their dogs, and they had found a private beach, very secluded, so they wouldn't get caught. She listened, and she remembered, and, like every other day, she went home.

Some time later, she was in her room, listening to music and reading. She didn't pay much attention to anything else going on in the house, so she was surprised when she heard a barking dog. She listened, and realized there were other noises too. People. Loud voices. She looked out her window and saw lights flashing. Red and blue. She saw people on the lawn. Her parents. People wearing uniforms. And a dog, in the back of a police car. She knew that dog. It was his dog. So she felt compelled to go see.

She went downstairs, and then outside. Her parents looked up at her approach. Her dad wanted her to go back inside. The people in the uniforms, police officers, started towards her. She backed away. She moved around them, towards the dog. She heard her mother saying, "She's autistic, she can't help you. She barely talks."

She shook her head at them. She knew how to talk, of course she did. She just never saw the point. No one wanted to listen to her anyway. But the dog...she approached it, and it tried to get out the window at her. She heard her parents in the background, arguing, and she ignored them. A hand reached out, and she startled back. But it was one of the police, a woman. She opened the door of the car and the dog jumped out. The girl sat on the ground and the dog jumped on her. She laughed, and stroked its fur. It licked at her. Then she noticed a shadow. She looked up. The woman was still there. The woman crouched down beside her.

"So you like dogs?" the woman asked. The girl thought about it. This was a police officer. Who was talking to her. She saw her parents watching them. They looked angry. And worried. The girl looked back at the policewoman. And nodded. "Your mom says you are autistic. You don't talk. But you can understand me?"

The girl looked back at her parents again. Nodded again. And then, not understanding why she wanted to explain, but feeling she should, she said, "It's called Asperger Syndrome. It's on the spectrum. Others have it worse than I do."

The policewoman looked surprised. "She said you don't talk!"

"Don't. Can. But don't."

"Then maybe you *can* help. Do you know this dog? He seems to like you."

The girl kept petting the dog. "I know who he belongs to. But we haven't met before. He's just friendly." She looked at her parents again. They looked shocked that she was talking.

The policewoman thought for a moment. "Well here's the thing. And tell me if you don't understand any of what I say. This dog was found running loose. He has no collar on him. We haven't been able to find out where he came from. But, when we found him, we also found another dog. That other dog was sick. Someone fed him something that was laced with drugs. So now we are trying to find out where they came from so we can make sure no one else is hurt. If a person ate the same thing the dog did they could be sick too. Do you understand?"

The girl bristled. "I'm not stupid. Just different. Are you mad?"

"At you? Of course not."

"No, at whoever made the dog sick. Are you mad?"

The policewoman blinked. "Oh. Do you mean will they get in trouble? I don't want you to worry about that. Maybe it was just an accident, right? But we do need to find them..."

The girl frowned. By telling what she knew, the boy could get in trouble, if he had anything to do with the sick dog. But his dog was here, and so he might be sick somewhere too. She looked at her parents. They nodded at her, encouraging her. They wanted her to tell. So she took a breath, and said, "I know where they are." She explained then, without looking away from the dog, what she heard about the party and where they were going. About the private beach, so no one could find them. She heard the other officer talking into his radio, telling everyone else what she said. She stopped talking then. She felt tears in her eyes. She buried her face in the dog's soft fur. She really hoped she didn't get anyone in trouble, especially not the boy.

Then the policewoman spoke again. "Thank you. We can find them now. You also said you knew who the dog's owner was. Can you tell us about that?"

The girl looked back up. Then she started telling them about the boy. After she had been speaking for a few minutes, she realized they were all staring at her. She trailed off mid-sentence and looked around at them. Her parents looked stunned, the police officers a little amused.

The policewoman then smiled and said, "You like that boy, don't you?" Without looking at her parents the girl nodded. "Tell you what. How about you look after the dog for a little while. We have to go help the others look for your classmates. When we find them we can come back for the dog. OK?" Again the girl nodded. She hugged the dog again. She heard her parents and the police officers talking, and then the officers left. Her parents tried to talk to her, but she was done talking now. So she just got up and took the dog inside.

Later on the policewoman came back. The girl was in her room with the dog, playing a game, and this time the policewoman came inside the room. The girl looked up at her. The policewoman sat down next to the girl. The girl said, "Are you going to take the dog away now?"

The policewoman shook her head. "Actually, I was hoping you'd be able to look after him for a while longer. You see, because of your help earlier we found your classmates. Most of them were OK. But a few of them were sick."

The girl thought for a minute. "Did they eat the same stuff as the other dog? That had the drugs?"

The policewoman shook her head. "They did not eat it, no. But they did take drugs. Some of them took too much. That is why they are sick. We had to take them to the hospital."

The girl looked back at the dog. "Did he — I mean, you know, the boy I told you about? Who owns this dog? Did he. . .is he sick? Is he one of them? And, if he is. . .will he be ok?" The girl was getting surprised at herself now. This was the most she had spoken for as long as she remembered. Mostly she just ignored everybody and lived in her stories, but. . .this talking thing wasn't actually so bad.

The policewoman nodded. "He is sick. But he should be ok. His parents are with him, and dogs aren't allowed. I have to go back there in case he wakes up soon but I wanted to come and thank you for your help earlier."

The girl looked at the policewoman. "I will look after the dog. I hope the boy is ok." Then she started playing her game again. The policewoman seemed to understand that the girl needed her space, and she left.

Eventually, the boy came back for his dog. He never told the girl that when he woke up from his accidental overdose, the policewoman was there. She told him how out of control that party had been. She said that if it had not been for the girl they might not have found him in time. He never said how shocked and surprised he was to hear it, because he, like many of his friends, hadn't even realized that the girl could talk. He never told her how lucky he was that she remembered so much, that, in fact, her 'specialness' had probably saved his life. What he did say was, simply, "thanks." The girl smiled at him, and said, rather quietly, "you're welcome."

I would like to say that they became wonderful friends, and lived happily ever after, and all that, but let's face it, when does that happen outside of fairy tales? What did happen was this. The girl started to try and make more of an attempt to talk to people, but people who knew her were so surprised by this that she was often embarrassed by their shock. Her attempts proved more successful when she went to college and most people there didn't know her at all or anything about her. It also got easier when she discovered the internet and realized that she could talk to people without actually speaking to them. She did also get her own dog as soon as her parents would let her.

The boy was friendly towards the girl after that, and it was actually he who introduced her to the internet. They kept in touch after that through email and he discovered she was actually quite funny. And smart. They do remain friends, and as they live in different towns it is likely that friends is all they will ever be.

Angels Among Us

By Lori Pearson

The angel in the dining room at the Ramada
did the "nothing up my sleeve routine" before he took his seat.
He let me know he noticed me and never let me go
through a warm roll, salad, steak and wine.
And then he came and said
"You must love her very much — she is beautiful" and left.
The waiter scratched his head and wondered if he stayed in
this hotel
for he did not linger to collect his bill
only to touch two souls
and eat.

IMBY

By Lori Pearson

It was a When-in-Rome moment, except it was not Rome but London and she was climbing the steps of a double-decker bus in the rain.

"Might as well go all the way," she thought, making her way to the front row, where she knew she would get soaked, but where the view would be the best. The iconic double decker red bus in London had an enclosed bottom level and an open air top one. It consisted of two banks of seating, separated by an aisle. She chose the left front row as the right was already occupied.

Opposite her sat a rather well-dressed man in a formal, dark suit. With the nervousness of a first time traveller, she turned to him, feeling that he must be feeling something similar to what she was and she wanted to share the moment.

Scintillating conversationalist that she was not, she turned to him, asking "Is this your first time in London?"

The man turned; his face was ravaged with scars, three stripes across each cheek, precisely placed. His soft voice, a cultured voice, answered that he had been educated in London and had returned as a guest of the British government.

"Where are you from?" she asked.

"The Sudan," he replied.

She nervously searched her memory banks to determine if she knew anything about the Sudan. Her Ontario education had made history or geography mandatory for only one year and she had chosen history. She had heard of the Sudan, but it was only a name. She could root out nothing further in her memory.

"Canada," she stated. She wondered if he had heard of it. "Ah, yes", he replied. "I studied Canada in school."

She flushed. What did I learn in school? she wondered. Her mind flashed on the narrow scope of her educational journey. She had learned what she needed to put context to where she was and little more.

And so the conversation began. She learned that the scars on his face were tribal markings. He said that he was the last of his family to be marked in this way. He explained the markings were comparable to surnames.

He said that in his country people had land but no food. She babbled about the shift to organic food production in Canada and he sighed, saying that this was a luxury of people who already had the technology to produce enough food.

He spoke of his time in England, and his university education, which he felt was a most reverent gift. He spoke of his nostalgic return to London with overwhelming gratitude.

He spoke with no sense of self-pity of the plight of the Sudanese. She shifted uncomfortably in her seat. In Canada, she lived in poverty, living on social assistance in government-assisted housing; she owned a car. She began to suspect that her perceptions of herself were a sham. She was a social activist, an advocate for improvements to the social safety net. She viewed her own government as oppressive in terms of how issues like poverty, mental health, family violence, child welfare etc. were handled. She viewed the coverage of basic needs as a right of citizenship.

She saw nothing of the tour, she did not feel the rain, as all that she could see was a glimpse of something beyond what she knew and understood.

She got home from her trip, a once in a lifetime journey made possible by compensation for an injury she had experienced. She looked up the Sudan.

She flinched.

Why don't I watch the news? she wailed internally while realizing that unless it was in her own backyard it was as if it was unreal. She had been no ambassador for Canada on her trip – she had been an ambassador of ignorance.

Later that week she heard on the news that the IRA had detonated a bomb on the Strand. She had stayed at the Strand Palace Hotel.

The world changed irrevocably for her. The world had become her backyard.

The responsibility was overwhelming. When she watched the news, she cried. She could not really change her response to the rest of the world, but she could change the way she saw her role in it.

If I am going to be narrow-minded, she thought, then let me do it well and enhance that which is within my reach. And her life went on.

But almost every day she wondered if the man from the Sudan was okay. There was grief involved in this wondering – what she wouldn't give to speak to him again.

A Trickle of Words About Writer's Block

By Jocelyn MacLean

I've had writer's block for about a year. It sits like a shadow over me, an unwanted constant companion, replacing a well-loved friend, one I had known for years.

This has happened before, for days, weeks and moments. I've never been blocked for so long before. I sometimes wonder that when this dam breaks the rush of words will be overwhelming. I wonder if the lake of words will come out, making up for lost time.

My mind feels heavy with the remnants of cobwebs, and I rarely remember the end of the thought I've just begun. Perhaps it's the thought that I have no deadline to meet or that there's no automatic paycheque afterward that makes writing such a struggle. This feeling is foreign, and leaves me knowing I've lost a part of my mind that I may not regain.

I've put writing on my calendar. Cleared space on my desk and my timetable. As if a schedule is at the root of the problem. I've read prompts, great works, and silly poems. Yet I still come up empty each time I fire up the word processor, or place my pen against paper.

Sometimes I can force a trickle of words, but it's nothing akin to the torrent that used to flow from my mind. I feel helpless at the passage of time, I am at a loss to record my day-to-day life, and I feel like my missing words are a black spot on my personal history. These days are lost, not only in the passage of time, but for those in the future who might want to know.

I struggled through a month-long competition to write a novella. It was a mess, lacking in passion and embarrassingly tedious. It was a mind-numbing exercise in wasting time.

I fill the hours I used to spend crafting sentences, and creating characters, with staring at the ceiling and pretending nothing is amiss. The hours are lonely without the stories to keep me company. Without the consistent recording of |triumph and trouble.

When this time is over, when I find my voice again, I know I will be grateful. Grateful for the ease of communication, grateful for the company I prefer to keep, and grateful for a way to fill the lonely hours.

I've had writer's block for about a year now, and I seriously hope that it soon starts to ease.

Why You Are Loved

By Lori Pearson

You are harmony, a blending of voice and chord,
Experience and youth
Laughter and sorrow
Joy and hope and love and tenacity
The blending of all that is you
Creates love

You are more than harmony,
You are the laborious work of expression, arrangement
The way the notes dance on a staff
To be read into music
The brilliant dazzle of crescendo, diminuendo, andante, andante
A jolt of understanding to heart and soul
The music that is you
Creates love

You are more than music
You are the inspiration that in delight
Brought stick and rock into a rhythm of sound
Brought voice into catharsis
In communion with God
Your laugh on the breeze
The most beautiful refrain
The inspiration of who you are
Creates love

In the timelessness of forever
Before music, there was you
Waiting to be born to a world looking to rejoice
And with every breath, a song released
With every word, love set free
The light within your soul
A beacon to those along the way
The light within
Is always love.
For this and more
You are loved.

150 Word Topics

The highlight of each Oulipo gathering is hearing each other's take on what we call The Topic. The topic is something — a word, a phrase, a situation — that we decide upon at the end of each meeting. Then each of us goes away and writes a maximum of 150 words based on The Topic, and, when next we meet, reads out the result to the others. Here's a sample of some of them.

Voice on the Stair

By Ann Partridge

Editors Note: Whenever we handed out 150-word topics at the end of each meeting, we knew that Ann Partridge would return with three examples, each linked to one another. Here's an example of an imagination at work.

Voice on the stair 1

"What on earth?" Karen groaned, rubbing her eyes as she descended the stairs.

There was a parade of shoes across the hall. Upon further examination, what appeared to be every shoe, boot, sandal and slipper in the house had been placed heel-to-toe in a line that extended from the kitchen, through the dining room across the hall and ended in the living room where four-year-old Kira appeared hypnotized by the TV.

Karen considered ignoring the odd display because this was the only morning when she wasn't scurrying to get herself, Brian and the kids ready to leave. Kira, the youngest, was an early bird. Recently they had decided she could be trusted to get up and watch cartoons without mischief.

Finding the remote, Karen shut the TV off. "What made you do this with the shoes, Kira?" she asked her small daughter.

"The voice on the stair told me, Mama."

Voice on the stair 2

"Houston, we have a problem," Karen said.

"Not the Sunday shoe situation, Mrs. Houston?" Brian asked from behind his newspaper.

"Knives, Brian! This morning all our knives were laid

out in a star pattern on the hall floor."

Brian closed his newspaper. "Kira knows she's not allowed to use knives. She could have been hurt. What did she say?"

"The voice on the stair, again. I asked at school and daycare and they don't recall any story like that. I Googled TV listings for a cartoon and nothing comes up. We're going to have to take her to a counsellor or something because now it's. . ." Karen stopped the discussion when Kira and her nine-year-old sister Kelly entered the kitchen.

Brian studied his youngest daughter closely and thought she looked like an angel with her blond curls and wide blue eyes. Picturing her with sharp knives made his jaw ache.

Voice on the stair 3

The jerking motion of his head dropping suddenly startled Brian awake. He was sitting on the floor leaning up against the wall in the dark bedroom. Beside him, the door was open a crack and he was straining to hear the sound of his youngest daughter padding down the stairs. He wanted to witness Kira's odd behaviour and see if she looked like an automaton or what. This was the third morning and nothing had happened.

He heard the slight squeak of the girls' bedroom door. He should oil that hinge sometime. He peered out into the hall where a night light illuminated his baby girl. She held onto the railing and started down the stairs looking as sweet as ever.

He got to his feet and was about to open the door and lean over the railing to follow her progress when he heard the voice on the stair.

Voice on the stair 4

"Eggs. Place one egg on each step. Start at the top. You must obey the Voice on the Stair."

Brian stops himself flinging open the door and

confronting the voice. He decides to take a creative approach to the situation. He shakes Karen awake, whispering to her. He goes to the dresser where he finds a candle and matches. He rummages around and Karen can hear the sound of paper ripping. He leads her to the bedroom door and lights the candle and paper, yelling, "Fire! Everyone out!"

Opening the door, they see Kelly race out from her bedroom and start down the stairs.

"Eew, gross!" Kelly cries. She stops her descent and stares at her bare foot coated with egg. "Kira, look out! Forget the eggs, we have to get out!"

"But, the voice on the stair said," Kira answers obstinately.

"It was me, you dumb kid," Kelly confesses.

Siblings

By Carole Payne

I wish I could claim this story as my own, but it came to me from a past principal of Emmanuel College. We were talking about making funeral arrangements.

This reminded him, he said, that sometimes ministers have to bury people who have absolutely no redeeming qualities. This can cause unimaginable dilemmas when they have to deliver the eulogy. Doug recalled the story of one minister who could not, even with trying for three days, think of one nice thing to say about the person in the coffin before him. In desperation he looked around at the members of the sparse congregation gathered expectantly. "I invite any of you to say something about the deceased, " he said. There was an unbroken silence for what seemed like eternity itself. Then one small voice chimed in from the back of the church, "His brother was worse!"

By Michael Hanlon

Some years ago I gave a woman in her seventies a ride home from Tai Chi and she told me she lived alone except for weekends, when her brother came to stay.

"He's one of the little people," she said. "He has problems."

I saw them occasionally about town, he holding her

hand, starting with alarm at passing cars and even pedestrians. She was a roundish woman, not much more than five feet tall, he square-shaped and barely up to her shoulder.

Just the other day I saw them sitting on a bench, she, in her eighties now, leaning back and peeling an orange, he side on, following her movements. The orange peeled and quartered, she handed it to her brother who leaned back while she turned side on and watched him with joy and love and, perhaps, pride. It was a sweet moment for the three of us.

∞

By Laura MacCourt

Luck. The best kind, too. No other little sister has ever been happier.

He is my deepest confidante, earnest ally, advice bestower (asked or otherwise), third parent, forever friend, board game opponent, and peppermint patty dispenser (as needed). He has made me laugh but, astoundingly, never cry. Here is the only other soul on earth who shares my uncheckable tendency to laugh at sorrowful news. Respectful we insist, yet frustrated at our untimely giddiness and display of truly unfelt mirth.

A rainbow, coloured beyond an artist's ken, best illustrates the scope of emotion and adventure that mere words fail to capture. A welcomed little sis, I appreciate all he has said or done (or attempted to say or do) in contributing to my life...

...which *must* end before his. All that I am or might be has his loving influence to thank. I don't call it "living" without my brother.

Time

By Ellen Curry

What is time?

Do you remember as a child, how the time between school holidays took forever?

As a teenager you tried to cram every minute of your time full of fun and activity.

A mother never finds enough time to do everything that's needed.

All of a sudden time passes so quickly that it's always either Friday or Monday, preparing for the weekend or just getting over one.

As a senior you make time for the things that are important to you and never mind the rest. You are retired now and you can spend the morning reading the paper with a cup of coffee or get yourself into your exercise routine early before you start the day. How shall I spend it? Nine holes of golf, lunch with friends that lasts two hours and then home for a read.

Time spent my way.

The Senses

By Laura MacCourt

Wagon rides into orchards are unhurried as the growth of trees. We disembark, brushing rough, barn-scented bits from our jeans, and pat the horses' smooth, shiny hides. Pleased, they toss leather-dressed manes, jingle silver bells, and mouth their metallic bits.

"Apples for you two later."

Orchards beckon tree by tree with round rosy-green fruit. Air is tinged with ripeness. Boughs are weighted, leafy and fruit-clad. Earth is spread with windfalls – soft, mushy, hard, shiny, spotted, nibbled, temptingly perfect.

The quick snap as an apple is parted from its tree is followed by lustful biting as a mouth experiences clean, crisp tartness. The most desired apple is just out of reach, yet we strain and climb, never taking our eyes off the prize. Our fingers clasp the orb, our nostrils swell to the scent of legions of apples hanging all about. Leaves, branches enveloped and apple-sotted.

This is our Eden.

By Mary Soni

Her senses were getting completely overwhelmed. The fierce wind whipped around her, chafing her skin. It tasted acrid in her mouth, and smelled worse than the worst thing she had ever encountered. The noise of it was a cross between the fiercest wind and angriest shouting imaginable. And she couldn't really see anything, because the wind had brought tears to her eyes. She had tried to brace herself. This was her job, after all, to be dealing with this stuff. But this. . .this was completely out of control. As she once again tried to calm herself, to try to tune out the chaos around her, and find that spot inside herself from which she could reach out and try to end it, she couldn't help but think to herself, "I hate pissed-off poltergeists!"

Starlight

By Michael Hanlon

First overnight stop on our trip out west. All well until just north of Lindsay, when Emily screams, "We have to turn back." I hit the brakes. "What for?" I ask, anxiously.

"She forgot her cell," Anna, 17, says. "She has to call Darrell (she stretches the name with a sneer) every hour to tell him she still loves him."

"I do not," says Emily, 13. "None of you understand."

Six snivelling hours later, we find the campsite. Perfect. Lake view, spectacular sunset ahead. Anna's helped Jane pitch the tents. I've peeled the potatoes; Joey, eleven, has fetched the water to cook them in. The stew we've brought with us is ready to be reheated.

But Emily is still sulking because I wouldn't stop and buy her a new phone.

"Listen, kiddo," I say, "Stop behaving like some pampered rock star. Light the damn fire."

Awaiting Evening's Peace

By Laura MacCourt

A slight zephyr stirred the tall grass prairie in late morning's sun. Already intense heat was affecting the sturdiness of wildflower stems. It was almost too hot for flowers.

Lilies, lupines, buttercups all sighed, resigning themselves to a blistering barrage of solar heat.

A wildly carved trail of flattened and bent stocks bore witness to a joyous dog's carefree romp earlier that morning.

Well concealed by lilac shrubs, branches of red maple, and densely tangled foliage, stood a large cement bird bath. Half full with fresh water that was quickly evaporating, it drew dozens of birds to sip, flap and linger. Happy, frenzied splashing would likely continue until the evaporation process was all but complete.

Infinitesimally smaller winged creatures either sought nourishment or satisfied another's need for it. Throughout the day, tiny wings buzzed and whirred until the moment of consumption silenced their efforts.

Evening's cool peace was hours away.

Arnold Raced From the Room

By Michael Hanlon

Arnold raced from the room. And being a Vietnamese pot-bellied pig, he made quite a comical show of it. Once he'd got through the door, he stopped and turned to gaze quizzically at us, head nodding slightly as though he were summing us up.

"He ain't finished yet," said Fritz, the Orono farmer who'd taken him in for a pet. As if on cue, Arnold raced back towards us and came as near to a screeching halt as a Vietnamese pot-bellied pig can expect to get. "He can keep this up all mornin'."

"Why?" my wife asked.

"Don't know, ma'am," Fritz said. "Don't speak Vietnamese so I never ast 'im."

"Perhaps he speaks French," I offered. "Pourquoi la hâte?" I said, addressing Arnold.

He, of course, snorted. And then he broke wind and wet the rug.

∞

By Laura MacCourt

"My dear, you're darling in ruffles. Let's try *again* to join these buckles across your tum-tum. That shimmering costume keeps bunching up. Your precious bonnet refuses to stay on. If I tighten that chin strap a...bit...more...there! That's not going anywhere now!

"Aren't these the dearest booties? I keep finding them here and there. They *belong* on your tootsies. Come here, love. Let's adjust those leg Velcros, snug as can be. *Snugger.* Hopefully no strands are caught this time. Alas, discomfort and haute couture are bedmates.

"Now...the eyewear. What a nose to balance those on. Transforming! Adorable seems so inadequate. Where's the camera? Stay right there."

A partially open door and a distracted mistress! In haste to regain his comfortable canine appearance, the dog didn't hesitate. Kicking off the intolerable booties, wincing as fur came with them, shaking his entire body, loosening straps and buckles everywhere, Arnold raced from the room.

Touch

By Mary Fleming

"You touch it."
"Not me, I'm not going to touch it."
The two boys looked at the seemingly dead squirrel lying in the middle of the road.
"Go on, touch it, I dare you; maybe it's still alive."
"Yeah, then what are we going to do?"
"You could take it home and make it better."
"Yeah, like that's going to happen; my mother freaks out if a mouse gets in the house."
"Well you could hide it in your bedroom, she'd never know."
"Ha, you know my mother, she'd know; she knows everything. Anyway, she'd blame you, she always does; then she'd phone your mother and boy then the sparks would fly."
"OK let me think; well, if it's dead we could bury it."
"Yeah but it might not be dead. How do you know when something is dead?"
"Well you touch it and if it doesn't move – it's dead."
"OK then, you touch it. . ."

∞

By Mary Soni

Touch is one of the most powerful of the five senses. It can evoke pleasure, or pain, it can make someone feel safe, and comforted, or scared, and alone. Because of this, it is also one of the most (if not the most) complicated of the senses. A hand raised in anger triggers a far different reaction from a gentle, loving caress. Touch can be even more complicated when one has survived some form of abuse. In survivors, touch can be like walking across a land-mine-infested battle field, because there is always a danger of setting off a storm of emotions and flashbacks. No matter how innocent a touch can be, the survivor will often view it as potentially threatening, or suspicious. With time and patience, however, touch can be re-learned as one of the most wonderful things two people can share.

On Choosing a Name

By Jocelyn MacLean

My mother spent a great deal of time choosing a name for each of her children. She grew up a Heather in the seventies and eighties, a name that did not really stand out as something special. I came first, Jocelyn Kathleen Marie. A very pretty name, if I say so myself. My great aunt visited us in the hospital, peeved at my mother. Apparently my cousin's first name is Jocelyn, although everyone called her Caprice. Figure that out. They mended fences and forgot the annoyance; there was a baby to gawk at after all. When my sister was born, my mom thought this was a second chance at the perfect name, Robin Alexandria. The phone rang the morning after Allie's birth, "Thanks for naming your kid after me," crackled across the line. Who knew that Uncle Bob was Robert Alexander.

By Michael Hanlon

"Grandmama rather likes George," he said.
"After her father," she offered.
"And the five who went before him, I suppose," he countered.
"I suppose we can't disobey," she conceded. "Any others on the preferred list?"
"Well, there'll probably have to be Edward, though the last one rather let the firm down. And perhaps Henry, we

haven't had one of those for a while."

"Bruce?" she wondered.

"Bruce?" he mused. "Might go down well with the Aussies. But they're not too keen on us at the moment."

"Michael then?"

"Michael?"

"After my father. You know. Him."

"What if it's a girl?" he put in.

"Or twins," she said. "The Daily Mail said there might be twins."

"I don't know if we could afford twins," he said. "They're getting a bit touchy about the purse, you know."

"Haven't we a spare palace we could sell?" she suggested.

The Traveler

By Margaret Bain

We do a lot of it these days, don't we – travelling, I mean. Highways are rivers of cars, airports seething anthills. In days gone by, Marco Polo didn't have much company on his epic journeys to Persia and China, rich young 18th-century Englishmen doing the Grand Tour of Europe travelled in style, but as an elite few. Now the traveller is one of legions, enduring security checks, nose-to-knees seating, discourteous staff frazzled by sheer numbers. But there is still, sometimes, a magic moment. A wild electric storm over Miami, the plane to Lima missed, a night in Cuzco punctuated by rattling gunfire – just a celebration, the nervous front desk said, but in the streets the policemen walked in threes. Then, next morning, the only traveller in a fify-foot dugout canoe floating down the Madre de Dios River, clouds of ghostly Sand-coloured Nightjars spiralling from the mudflats – priceless!

Breakfast with Charles

By Laura MacCourt

I had the most unsettling dream last night. So visual and intense that, on waking, I truly believed I had been there, experiencing all the horror and finality.

Now, having to face *him* across the table, the arrogant mumbler who seldom looks up, then dashes off, my stomach lurches. Tensely, I, too, hurry through my tea to distance myself from this man. Husband publicly, but there are three of us in this marriage.

Oh dear! Another flashback to that dream. Evening, acceleration, shouting. Then an *awful* screeching, all of us tossed about like ragdolls. Finally, only darkness, silence and tears. My tears.

Will someone help me? So much pain, everywhere! I can't free myself. It's worsening...my boys...tell them Mummy loves them...tell them to be brave...*William...Harry...*

I glance up. He is looking at me. Charles is actually smiling, just a bit, yet his smile does not reach his eyes.

Suspect One

By Christine Sharp

"Roll up the rim" time, Tim Hortons was crowded, so it was no surprise when Insp. Malenfant, a nodding acquaintance, slid into the seat opposite her. She gathered up her panini wrapper, used serviettes, and flattened coffee cup (she'd won a donut) and stacked them onto her serving tray to give him some space.

"Heard about Devereaux?" he said.

"Couldn't have happened to a more deserving guy."

"Whoever did it was powerful angry. The walls were drenched in blood."

"He had enemies. For good reason."

"Still," said Malenfant, dunking a Timbit® into his double-double.

She shrugged, stood up and reached for the tray.

"Leave it," said Malenfant, balling up a serviette and adding it to her pile. "I'll put it away."

She stopped at the exit. *Damn. Forgot my cup!* She turned and there was Malenfant, pocketing the thing. *Is he that frigging desperate for a free—.* She froze.

By Lori Pearson

Urine trickled involuntarily down my leg. Momentarily, I regressed to the sleepy warmth and comfort of the last time I wet my bed. Release.

Then, jolted to awareness of where I was in time, the realization, shame, craving for a cigarette so strong in me that I forgot the feel of soft flesh torn open, suffocating fear, dry heaves, the brokenness that can never heal.

Running, flight in darkness, pounding feet, ragged breathing, away or to, haven or hell? Rain or tears, leaves crunching underfoot or the crackling fire within of dreams incinerating. Panic, loss. Death?

It's cyclical, that homing device within that brings me to this temple again and again. Sacrificial lamb, exsanguinated, now forced to burn, incense on the altar, innocence on the block.

Numbly defeated, there rings in my ear, the sound of a voice, somehow not my own flatly proclaiming "Suspect One."

Ides of March

By Ann Partridge

Bru is the patriarch of the Ides family. An energetic 72, he is remarkably fit and a shining example of the effectiveness of Cambridgeshire's famous Inns-Ides-Out Spa. He lost his long-time partner and wife, June, earlier this year in the cruise-ship disaster off the coast of Italy. The family was devastated by June's loss, but as son Marc says, the healing must be done.

Marc and his wife Julie are responsible for the day-to-day operations of the spa and overseeing the use of *March's Magic Grotto™*. For those who haven't been submersed in the Warm Blanket Mineral Springs, the name refers to the bliss of a warm blanket after a hospital procedure.

Marc and Julie's daughters Cassie and Gay are the newest family members to join the business. Certified massage therapists and Reiki masters, they are the third generation of Ides at the Inns-Ides-Out Spa in March, Cambridgeshire.

Lullaby of Snow

By Laura MacCourt

Sleep. Truly the final nail in my coffin. A passage from night to day. Swift passage, I pray, but passage certain enough. Long has my body ceased to shiver, strived to achieve heat, fought the slow, terrible ache that now possesses every part of me. First came the wisps of powder high above, descending rapidly like crystalline fireworks. Next came the thunderous chorus of thousands of tons of dislodged snow, hurtling towards us. Mesmerizing, really. Unavoidable, certainly. A collision course we had not registered for, yet the possibility of death registered quite swiftly.

Are my comrades buried nearby, still breathing, still thinking, fighting the easy choice to lose consciousness for eternal peace? For that is what a fleeting nap, weakly yielding to the lullaby of snow, will bring. Sunny and windless, our day began. Schussing through untraversed mounds of brilliant white snow, we ignored earlier warnings. We knew best.

The Girl in the Emerald Bikini
A Progressive Story

This is a story written in a round by members of the Oulipo group. Each member wrote a short segment to further the story.

Michael Hanlon We were sitting in the back room at Nellie's when the redhead in the emerald bikini walked in off the beach and up to our table.

"Which of you gentlemen is Joe Chambers?" she asked.

"I am," we replied. To be honest, we were both lying.

Chuck stood and put out his hand. "Eddie Mars," he said. "This here's Violets McGee."

"And I'm Marie of Roumania," she said. "Nice to meet you both." She undulated into a chair, took a deep breath and pouted. I could swear Chuck whimpered.

"I was told Mr. Chambers could always be found here, in this back room, with a scotch. Which, if I'm not mistaken, Mr. Mars is drinking."

Chuck clutched his glass to his chest. "You got me wrong, Marie," he said. "This ain't Joe's. This here's my very own libation. Steve bought it for me."

Lori Pearson Only Chuck could carry off pretention over the blended "libation" he insisted on drinking, believing that a man with a scotch was even sexier than the shaken-not-stirred image of Sean Connery as Bond. Give him a redhead in a bikini and his peaty pheromones kicked into overdrive. If "Marie" was looking for Joe, Chuck didn't stand a chance. Joe's pheromones smelled of money and I sensed from the sashay of hips as Marie approached that she was a woman driven to the pursuit of success, most favorably someone else's.

Recovering my social graces and out of the deepest respect for the way she wore that emerald bikini, I held up my G&T and asked with a playful nonchalance I did not feel, "What's your poison?"

Marie started and turned pale. Chuck's face spoke volumes.

Christine Sharp　She stood up abruptly, planted her fists on her sharp hips and said, "If you two think you're amusing, you are sorely mistaken."

Before Chuck or I could respond, she thrust her forefinger at my face and said, "I was acquitted. And that's the end of it."

She glared at us, expecting something. I was too stunned to reply. "Ugh!" she flicked her hands at us, as if shaking off dirty water.

"You fools disgust me. Tell Joe I need the payment up front and in full." She turned and stomped away – as much as someone in flip-flops could stomp.

Chuck smirked as he sipped his drink.

The bastard, I thought. *I knew I recognized that look on his face. So much for a golf vacation. He knows what's going on. He's using me as his beard yet again. Well, I'm tired of playing the dupe, even for Chuck.*

Heidi Croot Maybe it's time we switched roles. I like thinking about Chuck as dupe, like it a lot. He's due, the prick. If I'm Violets McGee, he's that perfect asshole Simon Rosenthal. Bring on the shattered kneecaps. Gotta thank Chuck for sticking me with detective Violets. Inspired: that's what that was. "Justice will be done": wasn't that Chandler's anthem?

Chuck was still sitting there, fool grin on his face, making me madder. And then it came to me in a blaze of emerald green. Oldest trick in the book. "So how'd Joe get her off the rap?" I asked, scowling into my G&T.

"Joe tell you this?" Chuck asked in surprise.

Got him. "Sure," I replied.

He looked at me hard, and I met it, eyes mean, drawing down my mouth, the way Violets did it.

"By the way," I said. "That bitch Marie? She wants you. I can always tell."

Ann Partridge The eager look he couldn't cover convinced me this was the perfect distraction. "You think?" he asked with a lazy shrug.

I raised one eyebrow and nodded. Didn't want to overplay the angle.

"So Joe didn't dish the dirt?" Chuck asked.

I sipped my G&T and then shook my head.

"The law said the dame done in her old man."

I nodded like I knew.

"She ain't called Marie. Her old man was

a bookie."

I looked at Chuck calmly while I processed the facts and figured how I could use them.

"Joe and her went through the bookie's books and come up with goods on the cops, DA and even the judge. They couldn't touch her without doin' themselves in. See?"

I did see. So, Joe owes her a payment. . .

"Let's take Red a message from Joe," I said.

Chuck furrowed his forehead, but his eyes lit up.

Jocelyn MacLean

We paid the tab and left the bar. Red seemed like a gal accustomed to the finer things, so we made our way to the high-rollers' suites. We grabbed a discarded room service tray on our way up – it's best to have a reason to knock on the wrong door.

It took us four tries, but we finally had a glimpse of red hair as a door slammed in our faces.

Chuck knocked again. "Room service, ma'am. We need your signature." He lowered his voice, "I can't believe this broad opened the door for us, she really needs to go back to Hiding Out 101."

I chuckled, and tried not to show just how uncomfortable I was.

Chuck got a little more impatient and tried the door handle. He had to know this was a fruitless effort. He stepped back to take a little run at the door.

Carole Payne

"What the f. . .?"

Red had pulled the bolt and turned the handle. I glimpsed the hair as she poked her head out to see what room service had brought – this just as Chuck's frame hit the door. He burst into the room. As he swore in surprise, she screamed in a high tiny voice that was perfectly in synch with her sexy high heels. Those shoes were what I saw coming towards me as the two of them tangled in an unexpected heap half in and half out of that fancy door.

    I've got to give it to Chuck. He could have acted all professional, but not our Chuck. As I stayed out of the way of those heels, with the two of them thrashing about, he thrust his face close to hers and kissed her on that oh-so-sensuous mouth. She instantly shut up and stopped kicking.

Laura MacCourt You have to understand my type of guy. I never get the girl, but if someone else does, I sure like to watch...and as I watched, something wasn't right. This dame had red hair all right, but she wasn't the dame from downstairs. Could've been her twin.

    Hey, wait a minute! I'll bet they *are* twins. That's how they get away with whatever they choose to get away with. Two virtually identical babes that can be in two places at once. They sure know how to wear their clothes well. Man, do they ever.

    Suddenly I stiffened. There was a knife at my throat, held by a very lovely hand. I tried to see behind me. For a second, I caught a glimpse of that unforgettable emerald bikini.

"Just step over those two and walk in. Sis and I need to decide whether to cut you in or cut your throats."

Margaret Bain

Did I ever feel like a sap.

But Chuck and me, we've been in tough spots before.

As I flipped the knife out of Marie's long, scarlet-tipped fingers with a vicious twist of her wrist, I saw Chuck neatly relieve Sis of the sweet little Derringer she'd somehow stashed in that blink-and-you'd-miss-it teenie-weenie green bikini.

The two carbon-copy redheads glared and spat at us like frustrated alley cats.

"Now girls – talk!" said Chuck, keeping a firm grip on shapely Sis. "Talk your pretty little heads off!"

"Why would we talk to you fucking deadbeats?" snarled Marie, cradling her mangled wrist.

Even her voice was red-hot, but her eyes shifted just a tad.

"Look out, Chuck!" I yelled, just in time for him to dodge the lethal stiletto heel aimed at his jugular.

At that very moment, the door we'd crashed through smashed open again — and in came Joe...big, bad Joe...

Ellen Curry

"That's my girls, just like your big bro taught you," Joe said. "You harm one hair of either of my sisters and you'll both be planted in cement."

— 131 —

Marie turned to her sister. "Sis, give Joe the video of the President in bed."

"I left it on the night stand like you told me," Sis said.

That's when Joe started to get mad at the sisters. "All right, girls, stop fooling around," he barked. "Give it to me."

"Be sensible, Joe," Marie said. "How could I hide a video in a bikini?"

Chuck shook his head. "So you really thought you could scam the President?" he said.

Joe shrugged and turned and looked at the sisters. "Could have if these two had played it like I told them."

I looked at Chuck. He looked at the door. "Okay, they're ours," he said. "Come on in, boys, we got 'em."

About the Oulipo Writers

Margaret Bain

Most of my childhood was spent in India – Calcutta and Darjeeling – speaking Hindi, Bengali and Nepali, all these languages now locked in some part of my brain to which I've lost the key. Then school and university in Edinburgh and a drift southward to London, followed by immigration to Canada when the pyramidal promotion ladder stalled, and half our generation of young doctors left the UK. An intensely busy working life in Oshawa, long hours, little sleep, three dear children, and a growing interest in birding. March Breaks were (surprise!) in Arizona, Costa Rica, Venezuela. Farther afield, I've travelled in Africa, Thailand, Malaysia, Hong Kong, Australia, and most of South America. For fourteen years I was editor and co-publisher of *Birders Journal*, the only cross-Canada birding magazine, highly respected, but sadly discontinued in 2004. I still write regularly for several North American publications.

Moved to Cobourg in 1998 and love it here.

Heidi Croot

Words have been my sanctuary since I was a child. In eighth grade, I knocked myself sideways by winning the Kay Tatin Literary Award at M. B. McEachern Elementary School in my home town, Lambeth, Ontario, sealing the deal. Since then, I've filled a dozen thick journals and written odds and sods for my own pleasure, but the bulk of my relationship with words has been in the field of corporate communications, where I've been helping people connect the five essential dots of communication for more than thirty years.

In 2006, my husband and I quit our jobs on the same day and fled to the country, where I hung a freelance shingle. As principal of Croot Communications, I write magazine articles (once winning a best-feature-of-the-year award for a piece on the ethics of telling the truth to people with terminal illnesses), newsletters, brochures, annual reports, speeches, strategic plans, and the like.

But I'm about to flee again; it's time for something new. My question: has a lifetime of corporate writing snuffed the creative spark?

Oulipo and I are investigating.

Why I Write

By Heidi Croot

I write to still the kicking feet within, to give reason and its adversary an arena, to put the question mark to bed.

I write so that I can climb, in secret, the ladder of inference; let sharp, pointed things in and out; do violence on paper and not on the street; figure out what just happened (then "tell it slant"); expose an idea—the way a winter melt reveals the pathways embroidered by small, warm animals under the snow.

I write to confuse the black dog, turn a thought into a pillow, feel a mother's embrace, summon a wind from the west, leave my footprint for strangers. I write because I am not invented yet.

Mostly, I write in hope that the elusive, invisible hand will take over my pen.

Ellen Curry

Ellen Curry was born in Africa — Rhodesia (Zimbabwe)

She left Africa in 1961, immigrating to Canada, with her husband, Brian, and two sons, Martin and David.

Worked as a Public School Secretary for eight years, then opened Innerspace Dive Store/School in Oshawa, Ontario. She operated the store and school for 10 years.

Retired, spends six months in Cobourg, On, Canada, and six months in Sun City, Arizona each year.

Passions: Reading, writing, golfing, working out, canoeing, hiking, bicycling, horseback riding, swimming and travelling.

Published:
Be Careful What You Think, Volumes I & II
Two children's books: *Yoppie My Pet Monkey* and *My Visit to Windreach Farm*
Stories in anthologies: *Wisdom of Old Soules, Friendships,* and *Oulipo Canada: Book One*
Booklet: *Aging? Not Me, Too Busy Enjoying Life*

Mary Fleming

Who is this Mary Fleming? In the 16th century, she was one of Mary Queen of Scots' ladies–in-waiting, one of her 'Four Marys.'

Another Mary Fleming, closer to home, was my grandmother. She was a great storyteller and as a child, I spent many hours either on her knee or at her feet listening to her tales. In fact, one day I told her that when I grew up and wrote stories, I would be Mary Fleming too. I liked the name and remembering my promise, Mary Fleming was reborn in Cobourg in the twentieth century.

Mary writes for the love of it and like most of the Oulipo gang, is an avid reader – of good writing.

This group gives us, among other things, an outlet for our creativity and as we read our stories to each other, a roomful of friendly, positive critics who are only interested in helping to improve our skills.

Michael Hanlon

Michael Hanlon is a retired journalist who lives in Cobourg. His favourite writers are Robert Louis Stevenson and Graham Greene, who were related, John Donne, Raymond Chandler, James Thurber, A.J. Liebling and William Hazlitt. He likes cooking, golf (though it doesn't like him), opera, Broadway show tunes and jazz and would give his right arm to be able to play like Oscar Peterson.

Why I Write

By Michael Hanlon

I've always written for money, ever since I became an apprentice reporter on the local weekly newspaper in Windsor, England, just in time to cover the funeral of King George VI, the father of our Queen.

I kept it up for fifty years, writing and editing for newspapers and magazines in Britain, Canada and the United States. It was a huge amount of fun, a huge amount of work and a huge amount of travel. I journeyed to more than sixty countries on all seven continents to commit journalism, all at others' expense. And it gave me a pretty good living.

As I write this, I ask myself why am I writing this when no one is paying me? I'm writing this because this is what we do in Oulipo, put words together, sometimes in the right order.

You're welcome.

Laura MacCourt

My love of writing has clearly possessed me at times, or departed for a season, only to return with renewed urgency. Throughout my life, it has taken many forms. My first "book" at age eight was a quaint "Adventures of Raggedy Ann and Andy." Yes, I know it has already been done, but this piece concerned *my* Raggedy Ann doll, who smiles at me still from her little rocking chair.

Schoolwork kept writing in an active tense. In high school, as editor of "The Timepiece" newsletter, I was fortunate to have an English teacher who waived the need to regularly submit assigned work, because he knew I would instead be handing in chapters – thirty in all – of a novel I was writing. My first ever play, one brave sheet in length, travelled from brain to page at that time as well.

Early adulthood saw dozens upon dozens of poems come rhyming out, and a couple of longer narratives, too. Thrice I tried to crack the Canadian Broadcasting Corporation, and submitted radio plays to "Morningside."

Little successes came now and then with published poetry and short stories, victories in short story contests, and surviving the "Three-Day Novel Contest," with a certificate to prove it. A daily journal, now decades in length, requires me to "fess up," and has been amazingly useful to recall where I was, who I was, when, and why.

Now, as a student once again, my writing hand seldom rests, but the subjects are fascinating, and Oulipo rounds out my writing day with very rewarding challenges. May this first book, a collection from our merry group, find a welcome place in your home, as the entire project has found in each of our hearts.

Why I Write

By Laura MacCourt

Why do I write? Because to *not* write is to fester, and festering is neither welcome nor pleasant. Recall the last splinter your body, likely a finger, was forced to house. An uninvited, irksome pest, yet not without some intelligence. It found a weakness in your armour of skin, did it not?

By writing, I attempt to rid myself of toxins of the mind, and whatsoever or whomsoever may have challenged that perfect peace we all seek, yet rarely find.

As the cunning splinter is eventually released back into the world, so the act of writing expels tension, doubt and fear, enabling peace, assurance and courage to nest and be properly nurtured.

If one cannot write due to the immediate lack of writing materials, one must memorize, or risk the festering of undesirable nesting material. Clutter within is not easily purged.

I therefore write to clear both mind and heart.

Jocelyn MacLean

Jocelyn is a transplant to Cobourg from the East Coast. She has been writing since her first scratching on the good coffee table. Career highlights include: editing her college newspaper, writing a (yes, an entire) wedding magazine, chronicling the adventures of her cat, Molly, and the infamous *I'm Running Away From Home Becus (sic) You Don't Love Me Anymore,* written in the second grade. Jocelyn also runs a small business, giving people a venue to self-publish their books without incurring a huge expense.

Ann Partridge

A life-long worshipper of the written word, Ann Partridge has published short fiction in four anthologies available on Amazon.ca. She successfully completed her third NaNoWriMo (National Novel Writing Month. November, for all you aspiring novelists that need motivation) – which means she has a couple of novels in the works. Ann and her husband live in Cobourg.

Why I Write

By Ann Partridge

A voracious reader, I love nothing better than to immerse myself in a good story. "Imitation being the sincerest form of flattery" explains my endless inspiration.

I think I express myself best in writing. Sometimes. Other times I struggle to make the words convey my meaning. When my perseverance pays off and I find the right combination of syllables to capture an idea, it is magic. With a simple rearrangement of letters and spaces, I can communicate a thought, picture or, on a good day, even a feeling.

When the words multiply to become a story, I feel transformed into a supreme being, a creator of lives, communities and even whole worlds. It is wondrous to create a character. Sometimes one surprises me by taking on a life of its own and steering the tale into uncharted waters. Then I just follow their lead on a miraculous journey. Supremely satisfying sorcery.

Carole Payne

Carole Payne is a bookbinder living in Port Hope.

Lori Pearson

Lori Pearson writes mainly poetry but has forayed into short stories and plays. *Daughter's Pride*, a play conceptualized and co-written by Lori, was produced and performed by a high school and a play on the life of St. Peter was produced and performed by an elementary school.

Lori has previously won first prize in a short story competition and also an honourable mention.

Lori is currently working on a non-fiction book.

Lori grew up in Welland and has lived in Northumberland County since the late 1980s.

Christine Sharp

Christine Sharp relocated to Cobourg in 2008, leaving behind a successful career in the music industry, as Vice President of The Frederick Harris Music Co., Limited, Canada's leading print music publisher, and Director of Marketing for RCM Examinations, positions that she held concurrently. Christine graduated with an MBA from the University of Western Ontario and an Honours B.A. in Creative Writing from York University. She enjoys live theatre and recently directed "The Trouble with Richard" and "The Kitchen Witches" for the Northumberland Players. She will be directing their spring 2014 production of "Agnes of God". She has an ARCT in Voice Performance from the Royal Conservatory of Music.

Mary Soni

Mary Soni is a long-time resident of Northumberland County. She has been an amateur writer for many years, writing both short stories and poetry. She has been lucky enough to have one of her stories published in an anthology published by Brazen Snake Books. She is also a member of a local writer's group called Oulipo. When she is not writing, she is a voracious reader, and an avid player of video games. Her exposure to the vast range of things she reads and games she plays helps her in her quest to keep coming up with new ideas, although she freely admits that most of them will likely never be written down. She has also worked for the last five years at a local retail clothing store. This has not generally been a source for her writing, although she does write a poem for the staff every Christmas.